BIG SKY WEDDING

BROTHERHOOD PROTECTORS WORLD

DELILA DEVLIN

BROTHERHOOD PROTECTORS

ORIGINAL SERIES BY ELLE JAMES

Brotherhood Protectors Series
Montana SEAL (#1)
Bride Protector SEAL (#2)
Montana D-Force (#3)
Cowboy D-Force (#4)
Montana Ranger (#5)
Montana Dog Soldier (#6)
Montana SEAL Daddy (#7)
Montana Ranger's Wedding Vow (#8)
Montana SEAL Undercover Daddy (#9)
Cape Cod SEAL Rescue (#10)
Montana SEAL Friendly Fire (#11)
Montana SEAL's Mail-Order Bride (#12)
SEAL Justice (#13)
Montana Rescue (Sleeper SEAL)
Hot SEAL Salty Dog (SEALs in Paradise)
Hot SEAL Hawaiian Nights (SEALs in Paradise)
Brotherhood Protectors Vol 1

CHAPTER 1

BEING a local celebrity had its perks, Reaper Stenberg mused. As a prime example, take the night clerk at the local Bear Lodge Motel...

He'd watched Reaper and his partner, Jamie Burke, enter the motel office, and his eyes immediately widened. "You're him! Reaper!" he said, pointing at him. And then his gaze swung to Jamie. "And you're Sky's woman."

Reaper smirked about that because the males of Montana Bounty Hunters tended to get the most name recognition and fan mail since the trailers for *Bounty Hunters of the Northwest* started showing up on Twitter and a national cable channel—with the exception of "Bounty Hunter Barbie", as the fans had dubbed Lacey Jones, because of her penchant for wearing pink and "The Essential Bounty-Hunting Makeup Box" she now sold on their website.

The clerk was only too happy to verify that one Carlito Brannigan was staying at his fine establishment. He even offered them the keys without them asking, or bribing, him to do so. He did ask that they wait just a minute while he switched his monitor to the surveillance system, because he wanted to record the takedown.

Jamie turned to Reaper and rolled her eyes but gave "Darius" her email so he could send her the link once he uploaded the recording onto YouTube. It would join a growing list of videos as people in this corner of Montana had begun filming the bounty hunters' daily appearances— both the mundane and the action-filled ones.

Yeah, their lives had changed a lot over the last few weeks. New bounty hunters were being recruited, along with an accountant and web/promotional guru. They'd purchased state-of-the-art security and surveillance equipment, and now that they had an upcoming, dedicated TV show, their blog had gone viral, boasting over a million views the first day they'd gone live. Not only was their website generating income, but bail bondsmen were sending them more leads as well because of their success rate.

If they hadn't had Lacey's skills for creating disguises, they might have found their jobs harder to do when they needed to work "under the radar". Plus, signing autographs and taking selfies with fans on the street was kind of embarrassing, but he couldn't complain about the paychecks. Between bounties and his first check from the show's production company, his bank account was sitting pretty.

"Damn, Reap, you daydreaming?" Jamie asked, slapping his abdomen with the back of her hand.

Musings shoved aside, he made his usual growly, grumpy noise, because he knew it pissed her off. Jamie was convinced he was a dyed-in-the-wool misogynist, that he had yet to accept that female bounty hunters could be equally as effective as their male counterparts. But she was wrong. He'd long since accepted the fact that Jamie was a better hunter than he was. She was smarter, kept her head together when shit went sideways, and could handle the biggest, meanest criminals without breaking her bones or getting herself shot. Things he couldn't claim. Fact was, he looked for opportunities to mix it up with dirtbags, while she looked for "clean" catches.

Reaper would never let her know how much he admired her gutsiness. A man had his pride to protect. And he'd never admit he acted differently when he partnered with his wife, Carly. Fact was, Reaper tended to forget Jamie was female, not that she wasn't hot, but she was so competent he had to think of her as one of the guys in order to let her do her thing. With Carly, he tended to be a little overprotective, which had gotten them into trouble a time or two because it was hard for him to let her out of his sight. He hovered like a mother hen.

With Jamie, he didn't watch his words either —cussing and insulting whenever the situation warranted. She didn't get pissy or look ready to cry—not that Carly ever teared up when he said the wrong things, but with Jamie, he could be as crude and rude as he wanted, and the worst that would happen would be her slamming a door on his face or elbowing his gut. Yeah, he guessed they were friends. Hell, she was his best friend.

The thought rang like a bell in his head. His *female* partner was his best friend.

"Goddamn," he muttered, then bumped into her when she halted in front of Room 23.

"Look, since you seem a little distracted," she whispered, "how about you head around the back of the building and make sure Carlito doesn't try to squeeze himself through a window."

Reaper frowned but gave her a nod and turned to retrace his steps, jogging because Darius was likely watching. Reaper didn't want him speeding up the recording on his YouTube video because he was dawdling and Darius thought viewers would get bored. He looked ridiculous when that happened.

When he rounded the building, he flicked on his Maglite and counted the back windows until he reached 23. "I'm in position," he said.

He heard pounding, then, "Carlito Branni-gan," she shouted into his earpiece, "open the door! Fugitive Recovery Agent, here. I'm gonna take you to jail." She pounded again, a sound he could hear at the back of the building, but Carlito didn't open the door, and the lights remained dark inside the room.

However, after a moment, he heard clattering on the other side of the window, and he quickly placed his back against the wall so Carlito wouldn't see him. "Think he's going for the window, or maybe hiding in the bathroom. Better use that key," he whispered.

"Roger." Then a second later, "Okay, I'm in," she said, just as quietly. "Room's clear. Bathroom door's locked." Banging sounded again, this time nearer. "Look, dipshit, you're not getting away. Just open the goddamn door!"

Reaper grinned. Jamie's vocabulary had grown more colorful over the months they'd worked together. She sounded fierce when she let go.

The window beside him slid open. A head appeared then arms extended, and Carlito must have made a little leap because his shoulders quickly cleared the ledge, but that was as far as he got.

Carlito grunted twice and placed his hands on the wall beneath him while wriggling his body, but it appeared he was stuck, his belly filling the opening and cinching his gut tightly.

Reaper couldn't help it. He laughed.

"What the fuck's so funny?" Jamie asked.

"Get that bathroom door lock picked, and you'll see," he drawled.

"Man, I can't breathe," Carlito said, gasping.

A moment later, Jamie said, "For fuck's sake. Seriously, Carlito. You're a cat burglar? How the hell did you scale a two-story house to break into the City Manager's place?"

Reaper wiped the smile off his face and stood in front of Carlito. He reached for the large man's shoulders. "You have to hold onto while I pull."

Carlito wrapped his arms around his neck.

Reaper hoped like hell Darius didn't have a camera surveilling the back of the motel, because Carlito hugging him was definitely not a good look. "You're gonna have to push him through from behind, Burke."

"Jesus. Carlito, if you fart, I swear to God I'm tasing your ass," she groused. "And have you ever met a squat? Your ass is as soft as my pillow. Okay, get ready to catch him, Reap."

Reaper's body shook with suppressed laughter, but when he felt Carlito's body shift, he pulled with everything he had. At last, the big man's body dislodged from the window, and Reaper backed up until Carlito's feet dropped to the ground.

Instantly, the man swayed and would have fallen but for his tight hold on Reaper's neck.

A flash of light nearly blinded him, and he scowled at Jamie who took another shot with her cellphone. When she lowered her phone, she grimaced. "Man, I don't know what you ate, Carlito, but holy hell," she said, waving a hand in the air.

Reaper gripped Carlito's arms, pulled them down, then quickly turned him to face away. He snapped cuffs around the other man's wrists then gave him a little shove. "Come on. We're headed to the detention center."

NEARLY TWO HOURS LATER, dawn broke on the horizon as they drove down the highway toward Bear Lodge. After they'd finished the paperwork at the jail, Jamie had gone silent again.

Reaper watched Jamie out of the corner of his eye. Since she'd returned from vacation with her fiancé, she'd been silent a lot. Well, except for the ruckus she'd made the morning she'd first arrived back at the agency. That morning, she'd stomped to her desk, tossed her "go bag" on the floor, and then aimed a scowl around the bullpen before saying, "Don't want to talk about it."

He'd been tempted to ask her about what, but Brian Cobb, the office manager, had given him a quick shake of his head. Whether he knew what had put the knot in her panties or not, Reaper couldn't be sure, but other than raising his eyebrows, he'd refrained from responding. He was rather proud of that fact. His wife Carly would have said he was "evolving,", but since she'd decided to duck work to finish writing her first Montana Bounty Hunters thriller, he'd forgotten to mention it. Now, he'd have to wait for praise after he got home.

"Soooo," he said, just to make some noise and remind her that she had a passenger sitting right there beside her.

She shook her head. "Still don't want to talk about it."

Reaper drummed his fingers on the dashboard. "How's Sky? I was surprised he didn't come in with you."

"Sky's working with Hank Patterson's people for the next little while."

He nodded. Maybe that was why she was pissed. Only that didn't really make sense since she liked Hank. Maybe she was pissed because she wasn't working with him, too. "Hank got a big op?"

"No clue. Didn't ask."

Her voice was clipped, a clear message she didn't want to continue this topic of conversation.

Reaper decided to ignore the heavy hint. "You two pick a venue for the wedding?"

He guessed he'd said the exact wrong thing because her brows lowered, and her lips pressed into narrow line. A little alarmed, he decided maybe he should zip his lips, because her expression didn't bode well.

After a moment, she slapped the steering wheel with her palm. "I would've been happy with a quickie at City Hall. But, *noooo*, he wants some big fucking production. Do you know how much it costs to rent the banquet hall at Cooper's Steakhouse?" It was a rhetorical question, because she didn't pause. "Damn near as much as this stupid ring," she said, holding up her left hand. "At least the ring will last a lifetime. And don't get me started on the church. I'm a lapsed Catholic. Do you know all the hoops the priest wants me to jump through before I can traipse down the aisle? Hell, I never even had my confirmation…"

Reaper shook his head. "Sounds complicated," he murmured. He didn't do complicated, so he could commiserate.

"Damn straight. And the expense! I'd just as soon blow ten grand on a damn vacation and have a tan that lasts longer than the ceremony."

"Sounds like you two didn't agree on much."

Her shoulders slumped. "He's…disappointed. And I think…maybe…I was a bit of a bitch about the whole thing. I think that's why he told Hank yes when he called with a job." She glanced at Reaper. "I think he regrets asking me to marry him."

Her eyes were glittering, which made him nervous. "Now, Jamie, Sky loves you. Remember? I was there when he popped the question. Never saw a man happier than when you said yes."

"But that was right after I almost got killed by that terrorist, Nozari, and we were both feeling pretty lucky…and the sex was…"

Reaper raised his hands. "TMI, babe."

"You know what I mean. We were both…"

"Happy?" he muttered helpfully.

"Yeah. I thought I was the luckiest girl in the world. We'd just reconnected. I'm mean, it felt like fate, seeing him again, here, after we'd met on the other side of the world. We had so much in common—both ex-military, our time together in the desert, our love of this place…" she said, waving her hand at the mountains in the distance.

Reaper didn't like heart-to-hearts. He wasn't any good at them, and getting in anyone else's business made him uncomfortable, but she was his friend, so he pushed away his discomfort and said, "Tell me something. Is this your first fight?"

She shifted in her seat. "We didn't really fight. There's been no yelling. At all. Hell, he's barely spoken to me in two days."

Jamie sounded so miserable he began to fear she'd cry a tear or two, and that would never do. Women's tears made him feel…itchy. Reaper cleared his throat. "You two sleeping in the same bed?"

She snorted. "Sleeping, yes. Doing the horizontal mambo, no."

He nodded, feeling like, for once, he was smarter than Jamie. "Well, that's your problem."

"What? Not having sex?"

"That's part of it. You need a good fight. A loud one. Not that you need to trade blows—that'd be abuse—but someone needs to break something, toss a lamp or a radio."

"That sounded kind of specific."

He winced. Carly had hurled a radio at his head the last time they'd had a tiff, but she'd aimed wide. "Point is, you need to let it all out—the frustration, the hurt feelings. Sky's got to forget he's a gentleman, and you need to forget you're a lady. Physically, you're both in your prime, and you've both been to war. Civility is just a mask. Forget about rules and don't worry about holes in the dry wall. Connect to the animal inside you. The fucking will follow naturally."

She snorted again, but this time her shoulders shook. "Jesus to be a fly on the wall when you and Carly have a blowout." She shot him a glance, a smile curving her lips.

He grinned. "Makeup sex is the best, partner. After that, neither of you will give a damn if you're married in a church or the County Line Bar."

She shook her head. "'Civility is just a mask.' When did you get so philosophical?"

"Carly doesn't let me get away with caveman talk. And because she's so damn smart, I feel challenged sometimes to surprise her." When Jamie started laughing, he did, too.

"Reaper, I'm damn glad Fetch made us partners."

"Me, too, babe. Me, too."

CHAPTER 2

BY THE TIME Jamie arrived home, it was still the early morning hours. A quarter moon shone low the horizon against a brightening sky. Tessa, Jamie's ex-military police dog, met her at the door when she tried to sneak in unnoticed. Having a dog kind of killed any chance of a stealthy entrance. She opened the door wider and signaled for Tessa to come outside, and then walked with her around the front yard while Tessa explored and then searched for just the right place to relieve herself. When she finished, she trotted back to Jamie, and Jamie went to a knee to give the dog a big hug. "You still love me, don't you, girl?"

"Jamie, I still love you, too," came Sky's deep,

sleep-thickened voice.

She glanced over her shoulder. Her beau, Skylar Reynolds, stood on the porch, wearing only a pair of unbuttoned blue jeans, and she swore she'd never seen anything so sexy in her life. Dark hair, storm-cloud blue-gray eyes, stubble on his square jaw. Inside, she sighed.

His expression was set, hard to read. His gaze searched her face. She guessed he was trying to gauge her mood. "I missed you," she whispered.

He stepped off the porch and strode toward her, stopping a foot away. She pushed up from the ground and leaned against his body when he reached for her.

"I'm sorry."

"I'm sorry."

Their glances met, but Jamie's fell away first. "Reaper says we should throw things at each other."

Sky's chest moved with his short laugh. "Did he now? He's offering relationship advice?"

She wrinkled her nose. "We spent a lot of time together on the road. You know him. He gets chatty."

"Men are such gossips," he murmured.

"That's what Lacey says, too."

They shared smiles, and then Sky's melted away as his gaze heated.

When his head bent toward hers, she rose on tiptoe to meet his kiss. He thrust his fingers into her hair, and his thumbs cradled her jaw. Even though she wasn't a delicate flower by any stretch of the imagination, the way he held her made her feel intensely feminine.

His mouth rubbed then rotated, drawing her lips along with his. When arousal made her gasp, he thrust his tongue between her lips, and she clutched his bare sides because her knees went a little weak.

When he broke away to draw a deep breath, she asked, "Do you have to be anywhere soon?"

His mouth twitched. "Are you asking if I have time to fuck you?"

Jamie wrinkled her nose. "Reaper must be rubbing off on you, too."

His eyes narrowed sexily. "Reaper best not be talkin' about fucking around my soon-to-be wife."

The word "wife" instinctively made her stiffen, but if Sky noticed, he didn't let on. He palmed her ass and gave it a squeeze. "We've got time. Come to bed."

"Will I kill the mood if I say I need a shower?"

"Don't care. I woke up like this," he said, rubbing an impressive erection against her belly. "But you weren't there."

She arched an eyebrow. "Guess, for once, my timing is impeccable."

Sky moved away but caught her hand inside his and led her inside the house. Tessa gave a whine but headed toward the kitchen and her food bowl. Once inside their bedroom, Sky stood still as she pulled off her clothing.

"You wouldn't believe the skip we caught," she said, remembering the moment she'd faced Carlito's ass and flailing legs. However unpleasant shoving him through the window had proven, her photo of their skip, looking as though he was swooning in Reaper's arms, was going on the bulletin board.

"You were with Reaper. I'm sure it was epic," he said, then bent to shove his jeans down his thighs.

Good Lord, she'd never tire of looking at the man when he was naked. Ripped from his shoulders to his toes, she was breathless by the time she kicked away her jeans and underwear.

Sky fell back onto the bed and placed his

hands behind his head as his gaze roamed her frame. She always felt like she came up short when she was nude, because she really wasn't all that special. Not tall and long-limbed, not slim enough. But the way his breaths accelerated as she crawled over the end of the bed toward him, and the way his cock jerked as it stood away from his body proved he was into her—and soon to be *way into her.*

Walking on her hands and knees, she paused when her face hovered over his groin and she breathed in his musky, masculine scent. Her heart thudded in her chest, its rhythm quickening, and she couldn't resist leaning down to swipe his balls with the flat of her tongue then trail the tip up his impressive length. Before she continued moving upward, she sucked him into her mouth and gave his cockhead a wet stroke of her tongue, but she was too desperate now to play with him.

Sky must have felt the same way, because he slipped his hands beneath her arms and hauled her up his body. "Do you really think I don't still love you?" he asked as he smoothed his hands over her back.

She gave an exaggerated groan. "We had two

weeks to get things done. It seemed like the harder we tried to find things we agreed about, the further apart we drifted."

His fingers clamped on the notches of her hips, and he moved her, lifting her over his cock. She wiggled until the tip nudged against her opening.

"We also spent a lot of time doing this."

"Because when we talked everything went to shit, but when we—"

He stroked upward, entering her, and her eyelids drifted downward.

"Here, like this," he whispered, "we communicate just fine, don't we, baby?"

"*Yessss*," she hissed as he stroked upward again. Flattening her hands on his chest, she pushed up and leaned backward, taking him further inside. Once he was as deep as could be, she began to circle her hips, dragging his cock around and around with her movements.

"Fuck, yeah," he muttered.

She ground against him, scraping her clit against hair and bone, exciting herself so much she forgot about pleasuring him.

Until he tweaked her nipple. "Now, that I

have your attention..." he said and arched an eyebrow.

"Sky...?" She slowed her movements.

He twisted both nipples hard. "Yes, baby?"

Her inner muscles squeezed around him. Moisture flooded her passage. "I need it fast."

Jamie gasped when he pushed her off his cock and to his side. He moved over her, his knees on either side of her body, and forced her to roll to her belly. Then he scooted down her thighs and molded her buttocks with his hands. He moved lower and placed kisses on her ass, followed by nips that made her jerk and sigh. When he pulled at her hips, she pushed up and raised herself.

His tongue slid between her folds, long luscious strokes followed by pointed thrusts inside her. Too much. Not enough. She widened her knees and sank her belly, inviting him to continue to play.

When his fingers slid inside her, she clutched the bedding and moaned. "More...oh, please..."

Two fingers, then three, thrust inside her, fucking her, while he flicked her clit with the tip of his tongue. When he rubbed his thick thumb against her asshole, she whimpered. "Fuck me, Sky. *Now. Fuck me!*"

His fingers withdrew, and then he was there, his hands clutching her hips, preventing movement as he nudged then slid his cock inside her. He pulled free, nearly all the way, then slowly pushed forward again. He repeated this pattern, letting her savor every inch of him as he sank over and over inside her slick channel.

"Jesus," he breathed. "I wish I could stay in this moment," he said with another long glide. "You're so wet, and I can feel you tremble inside."

She squeezed around him because she was ready for more. "Faster," she whispered, then pushed up, bracing her hands apart on the mattress. For added measure, she tossed back her hair and glanced behind her, giving him a pointed stare as a challenge.

His eyes narrowed, and his strokes shortened and sharpened, coming faster, harder. She turned away, pursing her lips to draw air in breathy huffs. As he rocked against her, the moisture he elicited from her pussy added an aural texture with lewd, slippery sounds that accompanied the sharp, staccato beats as his groin slapped against her flesh.

His movements quickened again, and she gave another whimper, this one followed by a moan as pleasure built inside her. "Almost there," she gasped.

Abruptly, he pulled free and pushed her to the mattress. Then he rolled her again. When he came down on top of her, she couldn't get her arms and legs around him fast enough. She was desperate to pull him inside her, ravenous for what he would give her.

His cock sank deep, and he thrust his arms beneath her, cradling her close to his body as he jerked his hips and gave her short, harsh strokes that heated up her channel. The rapid pounding forced out her breaths in sharp gusts. She reached for his buttocks and raked her fingernails over his hot skin. She reveled in the powerful flexes that drove him deep again and again, and then her back arched and her jaw sagged. Colors exploded behind her eyelids, and she gave a thready cry.

When his orgasm hit, she felt every jet of come bathe her channel in rhythmic pulses. Grateful for his efforts, she kissed his shoulder, his neck, the edge of his jaw. She hugged him with her arms and legs, wanting to keep his skin against hers, his cock deeply embedded. Only when they were like this did she feel as though they shared the same breath, the same mind.

Sky hugged her and tucked his face into the corner of her shoulder. "I love you."

"I love you." Like him, she didn't dare say more. She'd leave it at that. Because, for the moment, she knew that was all that mattered.

SKY PULLED a clean T-shirt over his head and followed the scent of fresh coffee. He hoped that after they'd touched the damn stars during sex that the tension haunting them of late had dissipated. He'd let Jamie shower in the master bathroom, while he'd taken one down the hallway. They'd grinned when he'd suggested it because they both knew he'd never get to work if he joined her.

He entered the kitchen, feeling relaxed but also a little guarded. He hated that he felt that way. Something had to change.

Her back was to him as she poured two cups. He slipped his arms around her and bent to kiss her shoulder. "I hate leaving you today."

She chuckled. "I still have to get some sleep. You'd just be watching me snore."

"You don't snore. Much."

She gently elbowed his gut. "Not nice."

"It's cute." He reached beyond her for his cup of coffee then moved away to lean against the counter. He took a sip as she closed her eyes and drank from her cup. "Shouldn't you be avoiding the caffeine? You have to sleep."

She opened her eyes and gave him a wink. "This is to make sure I can make it to the bed." After another sip and a satisfied hum, she locked her gaze with his. "So, you haven't mentioned what this job is that Hank wants you to do."

He frowned. "It's an escort job for some Norwegian tanker."

Her eyes narrowed. "Where?"

"Strait of Hormuz."

She was silent for a moment.

Sky hadn't traveled that far for work since they'd met. He hoped she wasn't reading more into this than the fact Hank needed him.

Her mouth thinned. "Are they worried about pirates or the Iranians?"

"Both."

"How many men is Hank sending?"

"Five. We'll be operating a skiff accompanying the tanker. Another outfit's providing security aboard the ship."

"I didn't know Hank did this sort of work."

He nodded. "He doesn't, or at least, not often, because there are plenty of European outfits who provide this sort of service, but since the US has been making noise about their warships no longer providing protection to international carriers…" He blew out a deep breath. "This gig's like a job interview. The insurance company hiring the Brotherhood Protectors will be assessing the team. So, it's not more than one or two runs through the Strait. I'd be in and out in less than a week."

She nodded. "I didn't expect that you'd be going so far away."

Sky locked his gaze with hers. "Look, I don't have to accept."

Jamie glanced at her coffee. "But he wants a crew of SEALs, right? Ones who've done this work when they were active. That's you," she said, shrugging. "I get why he wants you, and why you would want to go."

"Jamie…I know the timing sucks."

She waved a hand. "No, I promise I don't think this has anything to do with…us."

"It doesn't."

She swallowed. "How long before you leave?"

"I'd fly out to Qatar tomorrow." Sky hated how a curtain seemed to fall over her eyes. He sensed her pulling away, and by the way her hands moved, plucking at nonexistent lint on her T-shirt, he knew she was trying not to freak out. Jamie didn't freak out. She might panic inside, but she'd square her shoulders and power through any fear.

She cleared her throat. "Guess I better let you go. I imagine you and the team Hank's assembling have a lot to talk about."

"We do." He grasped the hand not holding her cup and interlaced his fingers with hers. "Walk with me outside?"

She nodded, placed her cup on the counter, then let him tug her out of the door to the front porch.

"Think we should sod the front yard?" he asked looking at the patchy grass. Not that he really gave a shit about the yard, but he wanted her to know he was serious about being here, with her.

"I like it natural. Just like it is."

"I could remove more rock, flatten the ground out a bit."

"Why?" she asked, turning her head to look at him.

"I was thinking about Reaper's koi pond."

Her eyebrows shot upward. "You want to sink a koi pond? You're as crazy as he is. Do you know how much propane they use to keep it heated in the winter?"

He grimaced. "A gazebo then?"

She tilted her head. "What's this all about?"

He shrugged. How could he explain that he was trying to come up with some romantic gesture? Something as crazy and cool as the pond Reaper had installed for Carly. A ridiculous folly, but something Carly still smiled about every time anyone mentioned her pond.

"Will I see you tonight?" He hated the thought of leaving tomorrow without spending the night lying beside her, even knowing he'd barely sleep. He never did before a mission. Still, anything could happen when he got back to that part of the world.

Tonight, he'd keep away from talk of the wedding, so there'd only be happy thoughts to sustain them both for the next while.

CHAPTER 3

JAMIE HAD Tessa on a long lead, letting the Malinois do her thing. They'd been following a trail for nearly half a mile, having left Anna Cummings' neighborhood in the outskirts of Libby. They now moved toward forested hills. The ten-year-old had been missing since the previous evening, over eighteen hours ago. Early this morning, Fetch Winter, the owner of Montana Bounty Hunters, called to tell her that she and Tessa had been requested, by name, to assist with the search by the sheriff in Libby.

Jamie hated the reason for her being pulled out of the office for the day but was also grateful for the break away from the goodhearted people she worked with. Since Sky had left on his current mission, they'd been doing their best to help her solve The Wedding Problem.

The ringleader of the effort was, of course, Lacey Jones. The woman hadn't met a party she didn't want to organize, and the thought of planning a wedding nearly had her salivating. Not that Lacey had been any more successful getting Jamie to commit to "colors" or a theme. She may have gotten the hint that Jamie wasn't on board with wedding plans when she'd asked Jamie where she wanted to post a registry, and she'd quipped, "PetSmart."

Well, she was in the field today, so she had a short reprieve. A deputy trailed her, crashing through the brush, but Jamie tuned him out, watching Tessa as her nose moved left to right. She'd lost the trail twenty feet back. Maybe she needed the scent refreshed.

Jamie dug the baggie with the little girl's nightgown balled inside. "Tessa, *fuss!*" she said, giving the German command for her to heel.

The dog ran back to her side and sat next to her with her body hugging Jamie's leg. Jamie knelt and unzipped the baggie, and then held it beneath Tessa's nose.

The dog sank her snout in the bag and

breathed.

Jamie pulled the baggie away, stuffed it back into the pocket of her jacket, then stood and unclipped the leash. Raising her arm, she pointed toward the trail. *"Voraus, such!"*

Tessa moved out, her nose once again searching for the girl's scent. When her nose sank to the dirt and her tail stiffened, Jamie prayed that she'd found it again.

Tessa moved quickly now, and Jamie had to sprint to keep up. The dog had found the trail, and by the Malinois' little whines, the trail was a good one, rich in scent. Hopefully, that meant fresh.

They climbed a hill covered in cottonwood and lodgepole pine trees. At the crest, Jamie paused to stare down into a dark ravine Tessa was rapidly approaching. It was deep with rocky ledges.

Tessa halted atop one ledge and barked.

Saying more prayers under her breath, Jamie raced downward, sliding sideways on the steep hillside until she reached her dog. "What did you find, girl?" she said, kneeling beside the Malinois to peer into the shadows below.

A splotch of white that didn't belong among

the gray rocks caught her eye. She searched for a safe way into the ravine and found a deep crevice with grasses she could hold onto and made her way down to the bottom.

"Anna? Sweetie? Are you here?" she said as she moved below the ledge where the deputy had joined Tessa. Beneath the ledge, she saw the little girl huddled, her arms around her bare legs.

She was dirty and tears streaked her cheeks. "Not supposed to talk to strangers," the little girl said.

"It's okay. I'm with the deputy," she said, not moving any closer but pointing upward.

The little girl moved from under the rock and stared up at the deputy and the dog. "That your dog?" she asked, wiping her tears with the back of her hand.

"Yes, that's Tessa. She found you."

"I got lost and fell down," the girl said, and looked at her knees which were scraped. "I couldn't climb back up."

"That's okay." She shrugged off her backpack and set it on the ground. "I have some water and a bandana. I can clean your knees. Are you thirsty?" She unclipped her canteen from her web belt and held it out to the girl.

Anna grabbed it, unscrewed the top, and took a long draw of the water before handing it back.

Jamie glanced up at the deputy. "How about you radio that we've found her. We'll need a rope."

While the deputy called to relay the news, Jamie pulled a bandana from the bottom of her bag, along with her small first-aid kit. Gunshots rang out in the distance, the signal that the girl had been found. She cleaned the girl's wounds and covered them in Neosporin and Band-Aids. "Hope you like Spiderman," she said, patting down the edges of the adhesive strip.

Sounds of more footsteps approaching could be heard in the distance. More heads poked over the edge of the little bluff. The end of a rope was lowered with a harness attached. While the team above worked to pull Anna upward, Jamie made her way back to the crevice and climbed, grabbing handfuls of grass until she reached on top. The little girl's father stood with Anna wrapped in his arms.

"The dog saved me," Anna said, pointing at Tessa. "What's her name?"

"She's Tessa, and she's my best friend," Jamie said, smiling proudly. "Want to meet her?"

. . .

LATE THAT AFTERNOON, Jamie entered the MBH office in Bear Lodge with Tessa beside her, both dirty but happy with how things had turned out. An EMT crew had taken Anna to the hospital to be examined, but other than mild dehydration, Anna was fine. Too many times, searches didn't end as well, so Jamie was feeling a little high when she strode in.

Brian sat in his wheelchair in front of his computer monitor, working on the Excel list of bounties they shared with the office in Kalispell. He glanced up and gave her a wide smile. "I heard. Congratulations!"

Jamie glanced around the empty office. "Everyone out hunting?"

Brian nodded. "Reaper, along with Lacey and Dagger, took the new guy, Quincy, with them to meet with a bail bondsman in White-fish. Their skip's charged with armed robbery and is part of some survivalist group up there. Dagger said if you're free, they might need Tessa because he was last seen fishing in the Flathead forest."

Hunting with Lacey wasn't what she wanted

right now. Maybe she could peel off with Quincy to "cover more ground."

"Hook, Cochise, and Animal are in Glacier," Brian continued. "They're looking for a poacher who didn't make his court date."

"Big bounties?"

Brian grinned. "One of the film crew was here this morning. Said he wanted to get some more wilderness footage with the crew."

"Is he hoping Animal will chase another bear?"

He chuckled. "Animal growled all the way out the door."

Jamie settled in chair and rolled it up beside Brian. "I have clothes in my vehicle. Guess a shower's going to have to wait. Anyone call?"

Brian shook his head. "Felicity's popping in this afternoon. We're going to work on the ops van tonight."

"Thought you two had it fully outfitted."

Brian smiled. "Just tweaking. We've had it out three times now. Every time we go, we have more ideas. She's bringing some railing for behind the driver's seat. Something that will make it easier and faster for me to get out of this chair and into the seat," he said, tapping the arm of his wheelchair. "She had her metal guy bending pipe, and she wants to make sure it fits."

"Gotcha."

Brian gave her glance. "Did you ever think you'd be here, doing this?"

"You mean, working as a bounty hunter with film crews up our asses? Getting famous?" She shook her head. "Not in a million years." She raised her eyebrows. "You know the producer wants to do a segment focused on you."

Brian grimaced. "I'm hoping it's more like brief cameos. They already have my voice on the radio."

"Yeah, but she thinks people would be totally into 'meeting' you—the guy who runs the ops."

"From a fucking wheelchair," he said, rolling his eyes.

"It's pretty special, Brian. There are lots of disabled folks out there, many of them vets, who need to see there's life after injury. What does Raydeen say about it? They want to include her and the Soldiers' Sanctuary in the episode, too." She pressed her lips to keep from grinning, because any mention of the beautiful physical therapist seemed to bother Brian.

His eyes narrowed. "No clue. Haven't spoken

with her, and Hook hasn't said."

"You still avoiding her?"

He grimaced. "I'm not avoiding her. I have work to do."

Jamie tilted her head. "When's the last time you attended a meeting at the sanctuary?"

He shrugged. "Shouldn't you be getting out on the road? It'll be after dark before you get to Whitefish as it is."

She placed her hand atop his and gave it a squeeze. "This place doesn't have to be your whole life, Brian. Yeah, you lost your legs, but you're so much more than two knobby-kneed appendages."

"I did not have knobby knees."

"No, your legs were fine." She cupped the side of his cheek. "You're still a handsome man. Raydeen seems interested. Don't let fear hold you back from moving on with your life." She didn't give him a chance to respond, standing quickly, then bending to kiss his cheek. "I'm outta here."

"Be safe," he mumbled.

"Always try. Worry about Reaper's ass. He's always getting into trouble."

His chuckles followed her out the door.

CHAPTER 4

SKY SAT in the back of the skiff beside "Boomer" Rayne, grateful for the breeze the boat stirred up because the sun was beating down and the temperature was well over a hundred degrees.

Conversation was necessarily brief and loud due to the sound of the boat's high-powered engine. This was their second run through the Strait of Hormuz, and they were drawing near the tip of the Omani Musandam Peninsula, which jutted into the narrow channel between Oman and Iran. The last run had gone off without a hitch. They'd only sighted fishing boats along the way. Their second run would be their last.

Once past the Strait, they'd escort the oil

tanker to the port in Mumbai, India, where they'd catch a plane back to the States.

Sky had enjoyed reconnecting with the guys he already knew well from the Brotherhood Protectors. Boomer, Maddog, Chuck, and Swede were all SEALs, ones he'd met while on active duty. Before they'd left Hank's place, they'd walked their way through every possible scenario, every way things could go sideways.

Sky and Boomer had experience repelling pirates off the coast of Somalia during escorts. This wasn't their first rodeo. All the men were battle tested. No one expected this mission to be a cakewalk, but they were ready for whatever came their way, whether it be underwater mines, pirates, or the Iranian Navy, which of late had been flexing its muscle, taking ships for ransom on the pretext of the ships edging into their waters.

On the flight to Qatar, Boomer had sat beside him. He'd shared pictures of his wife Daphne and their daughter Maya. Sky had shared pictures of Jamie, although they weren't needed. Boomer had seen the trailers for the show. All the guys had ribbed him about being famous and a sellout, but they'd congratulated him on finding a new home and someone he loved.

With Boomer, he'd mentioned the difficult time he'd had nailing down wedding plans with Jamie.

"She doesn't seem like the type to get cold feet," Boomer had said. "She seems like she knows her own mind. Hell, she's running that place with Reaper, so she must be solid. What are *her* biggest concerns?"

"She says weddings are a big waste of money."

Boomer raised his eyebrows. "They kind of are."

Sky frowned. "It's one day. A day for us to celebrate everything we've been through to be together. A celebration we can look back on with our kids. I don't want some ceremony in front of an Elvis impersonator or some stranger at City Hall. I want something we can be proud of."

Boomer nodded. "Has she said what's important to her? Break it down. Maybe you two aren't really all that far apart concerning what you want."

Sky thought for a minute then raised his hand to count off the things he knew. He lifted his thumb. "Well, she's not all that keen about a church wedding. Said she's not religious, although she does pray a lot when things go sideways."

"Don't we all...?" Boomer said, the corners of his mouth twitching.

He stuck out his index finger. "She doesn't see the point of a wedding dress." He scrunched his nose, remembering the scarcity inside her closet. "Heck, she doesn't own that many dresses. She's more comfortable in jeans and sweats."

"She's not fussy. I like her already."

Sky smiled. Yeah, Jamie wasn't fussy all right; she definitely wasn't afraid to get down and dirty. Another finger. "She doesn't want a big crowd. Just her friends."

Boomer nodded then raised an eyebrow. "Do you want a big crowd?"

Sky realized some of her points matched his. "Not really. I'm okay with just friends, but I'd like my dad and brother there."

"So, no wedding dress or tux. No big church wedding. Who does she want walking her down the aisle?"

Sky blew out a breath. "I can't get her to agree there ought to be an aisle, but my guess would be Fetch, the guy who owns the agency. He was her commander in the desert and gave her the job of running the Bear Lodge office. She looks up to him as a mentor and father figure."

"Does she want bridesmaids?"

Sky lowered his hand. This was getting complicated. And a little overwhelming, thinking about all the details—no wonder Jamie looked like she was being dragged through hell every time they sat down to plan. "No bridesmaids, although I'm sure Lacey will be disappointed—"

Boomer grinned. "You mean Bounty Hunter Barbie?"

Sky chuckled. "Yeah, but she's not as fluffy as she appears. The girl's smart as a whip."

"Does Jamie want anyone else standing up with her?"

"Maybe her best friends—her dog, Tessa, and Reaper."

Boomer grinned. "The dog, I understand, but Reaper? That big ugly Marine she works with?"

Sky shook his head. "Reaper's a little rough around the edges, and he drives her nuts, but yeah, they're pretty tight."

Boomer sat back. "So that covers it, right? Maybe a bouquet? Something simple?"

Sky nodded, realizing that he felt a lot less

intimidated. "I still don't have a place or a preacher."

"What about the agency's office?"

Sky looked at Boomer. "That's a damn fine idea. Then all I have to do is find someone to officiate." He felt lighter after finally running through the list. The wedding didn't have to be a big deal. Their getting married at all was.

The skiff bounced on the water.

Boomer reached out and touched his shoulder. "We've got company," he shouted over the engine noise.

Sky slipped off his sunglasses and lifted his mini-binoculars to watch as two green-painted vessels bore down on them. The men in the boat all wore green uniforms, and the Iranian flag snapped in the wind above them. "Shit."

He turned to Maddog, who was captaining the skiff. Maddog gave him a grim nod. He already had his radio out, communicating with the tanker.

"Hold on tight!" Maddog shouted to the crew aboard the skiff then maneuvered the boat, whipping it wildly in the wake of the big ship to cut off the Iranian vessels.

As they zigged and zagged between the boats,

every SEAL, other than Maddog, trained his weapon on the Iranian boats. The water cannons on the starboard side of the tanker began shooting long, fat streams of water in the direction of the Iranians.

Sky hunkered down behind a firing notch in the armored plating surrounding the back of the skiff, sighting on the closest boat. He hoped the Iranians were only playing a game of chicken, hoping to intimidate the tanker into surrendering.

However, the Norwegian company that had hired the team had been very specific in their instructions. They would rather lose the ship than hand over their cargo and their crew. They were unwilling to set a precedent of negotiating with the Iranians.

Moments stretched. Then the first vessel turned, and machinegun fire rattled, spitting rounds into the water twenty yards in front of them.

"Don't return their fire," Maddog shouted.

Sky understood. So long as they didn't hit the boat or one of their team, they had to assume this was just another act of intimidation.

The boat veered away, and Maddog steered

the skiff along the length of the tanker, just out of range of the water cannons, then turned sharply to intercept the second boat.

A loudspeaker sounded from the Iranian boat. "You have violated the sovereignty of the people of Iran. Put down your weapons and prepare to be boarded. We do not wish to harm you."

"Funny fucking way of showing it," Boomer muttered beside him.

Chuck manned the radio while Maddog made another zig-zagging maneuver between the boat and the tanker. When he lowered the mic, he shouted, "Tanker's holding steady. The captain's talking to them now, telling them they're dead wrong. We're in international waters. The Iranians don't appear to give a shit."

Sky continued to stare down his scope, watching the movement of the machine gunner on the Iranian ship. If he had to, he'd take him out.

"We're nearing the tip of the peninsula," Maddog shouted.

The "tip" was composed of eight separate islands, seven of which Iran controlled. But once they cleared them, they'd have smooth sailing through the Arabian Sea on their way to India.

The minutes ticked by, and then suddenly, the second boat pulled forward, heading straight their way.

Maddog steered right. As the back of the skiff faced the side of the Iranian boat, Sky watched as the machine gunner positioned near the rails turned his weapon to track them. "He's going to fire!"

"Hold yours," Maddog shouted.

Sky gritted his teeth, knowing the gunner was aiming right at him, that the distance was close enough the gunner could easily strafe the boat and, depending on the type of rounds he fired, pierce the armor protecting him, but he drew a deep breath, and then another.

He only had to live through the next few minutes, and then he'd be home free. He'd see Jamie again. Have a chance to make things right between them. Marry the girl.

Just a few minutes more.

CHAPTER 5

MELVIN WAKLEY WAS A LUCKY BASTARD. So far, the armed robber had managed to easily evade the team tracking him through the Flathead National Forest. Lacey and Quincy were in Whitefish, staking out Wakley's brother's house, just in case he managed to give them the slip in the woods and look for outside help. Jamie and Tessa were hoofing it in the forest with Reaper and Dagger.

Jamie stared down in disgust at the remnants of a campfire Wakley hadn't bothered putting out entirely, which was a shameful act in and of itself, given this was fire season in the forest. The fire had likely been burning for hours going by the size of the branch he'd lain across the firepit that was still glowing red between cracks of the charred exterior.

"We'll need water from the creek," Jamie said as she sat on a fallen log. She opened her pack, pulled out Tessa's collapsible bowl, and poured water from her canteen into it. Tessa lapped at the water then stretched out on the ground, resting on her side with her tongue lolling.

Jamie envied her. She wished she could strip off her boots and socks and truly take a load off her aching feet. The tongue-lolling might have been enjoyable, too, but Reaper was stomping through the woods with her, and after she'd blown up the photo of Carlito swooning his arms, she didn't trust that he wouldn't be looking for a little payback.

Reaper settled on the log beside her and blew out a breath that billowed his chiseled cheeks. "Bastard must be laughing up his sleeves at us. This camp is five miles from where we were two days ago. He's moving back and forth and forward, leading us in circles. Fucker."

Jamie gave him a tired smile. "Tessa's exhausted. The heat's getting to her. She needs a break."

"We all do. I figure we should head out of the

forest. Maybe call in some guys from Kalispell—Mace and his dog Taco, for sure. We could have them meet us at Polebridge."

"Damn, I hate knowing we're that far north. Think that's where he's heading? Canada? We should have Quincy and Lacey meet us in Polebridge." She pulled out her cellphone and powered up. Their elevation was high enough she had two bars. The phone dinged six or seven times. She'd had calls. She quickly looked at her list of recent calls and saw Hank Patterson's number listed twice.

Hank had called. Why hadn't Sky? He should have been on a plane home by now. Had something happened?

She stood.

Tessa rolled her head to look at her.

"You stay, girl."

"Anything wrong, Jamie?" Reaper said.

"I don't know. I have to make a call." She walked away, passing Dagger coming into the clearing with a big bowl of water for the fire.

When she was far enough away for privacy, she took a deep breath and dialed Hank's number.

Hank picked up on the first ring. "Jamie, I've been trying to reach you."

Her hand tightened on the phone. "Was there a reason you were calling, Hank?"

"Oh, sweetheart, didn't mean to worry you. Sky told me to relay a message. Said he wasn't hurt bad, broke his phone, otherwise he would have called."

The heat must be why she was swaying on her feet. "What do you mean he's not hurt bad?" she said, speaking slowly.

"Said it's nothing that will keep him from making his flight. But that was three days ago."

"Hank…?"

"Sorry, one of the kids is crawling on my shoulders. He's fine. He's coming. He didn't want you to worry, and now, I've made you worry. Sorry about that."

She drew a deep breath. "Men. I swear. You're the worst communicators."

"Have to take another call. I'll let you know when I hear from him again."

The call ended, and she stood still for a moment. A breeze lifted the hair framing her face, cooling her skin. No, she felt clammy, like she could throw up.

Said he wasn't hurt bad...

What the hell did that mean? She kept her back to the clearing while she tried to get her head straight. Then she turned abruptly on her heel and walked back to the two men who were eyeing her with concern.

"We've dawdled long enough," she said. "Dagger, set the GPS for Polebridge. We're getting the hell out of these woods." She made her way to Tessa. She poured more water and directed the dog's attention to it, pointing a finger toward the bowl. Tessa lapped more water then glanced up at Jamie. She was ready. Whatever Jamie wanted or needed, Tessa would give her a hundred percent. Why couldn't people be more like dogs?

She packed away the bowl and her canteen, then stood and said, *"Fuss,"* bringing Tessa against her side. When she looked at Dagger, he gave her a nod and turned, heading straight into the woods again, heading north.

"How long until we get there?" she called out to him.

"If we set a good pace, just before dinnertime."

Reaper walked up beside her. "You okay?"

"I'm fine." Sky wasn't, but she wouldn't know anything more until she talked to him herself.

"You get some bad news?"

She shot him a glance. "Don't know. Sky relayed word to Hank that he wasn't hurt bad. That's it. Not, I've been shot. I broke my arm. My skiff hit an underwater mine, and I lost a leg. Just, 'I'm not hurt bad'. What the hell am I supposed to do with that?"

Reaper raised both eyebrows. "Sounds to me like he's not hurt bad."

Jamie made a face. "Men!"

NEARING SIX O'CLOCK, they exited the forest onto Route 486, just south of Polebridge. Walking single file alongside the road, they followed it into town. They met Quincy and Lacey in the parking lot of the Polebridge Mercantile.

Quincy looked relieved to see them, and the men shared fist bumps. Lacey looked as though she'd just stepped out of a beauty salon, not single strand of hair straggled from her pale blonde French braid, and her makeup looked nonexistent, which meant she'd likely spent an hour blending it onto her porcelain skin.

Jamie couldn't begrudge Lacey her perfection. "Don't you look cute," she said, eyeing her jeans that ended in crocheted cuffs at her boots and her pale pink, long sleeve Henley. Her fingers gleamed with a row of silver rings covering every finger, with moonstones and pretty little pearls at their centers.

Beside her, Jamie knew she looked worse for wear. She'd pulled back her own hair into a tight ponytail to keep it from straggling around her face, and her skin felt tight, so she knew she had a sunburn. Plus, she knew that the bird baths she'd given herself hadn't been enough to take the trail funk off her skin.

Lacey gave her a hug anyway. She was like that. Never judged. Or when she judged, she did it with the intent to make things better. When she pulled back, she said, "We've already talked to Fetch. His guys will be here at O-dark-thirty tomorrow." She rolled her eyes. "I don't know how to set an alarm for that, but I'm imagining they'll be here sometime before dawn. I've booked three cabins nearby, and Quincy and I stocked the kitchenettes with ready-made meals for dinner tonight and some easy breakfast foods for the morning. It's nothing fancy—a bed, a tiny kitchen, and a bathroom—but there's really not much here unless you wanted to go further afield to Whitefish."

Jamie waved a hand. "You had me at bathroom. Thank you."

"Well, we should load up," she said. "Here are your keys." She gave one to Reaper. "You'll have to bunk with Quincy." She handed a key to Jamie and gave her a waggle of her eyebrows.

Jamie didn't know what to make of that look, but she climbed into the back of the agency's Expedition with Tessa while dreams of soaking in a real tub played in her mind.

Five minutes later, they pulled up to a strip of tiny rustic log cabins.

Jamie glanced at Reaper. "We should probably meet later to talk about next steps."

Reaper shook his head. "You rest up. I'll talk with Fetch and see what he thinks. Make sure Tessa gets a soft pillow. She deserves it."

Jamie was too tired to argue. She looked at her key fob and headed in the direction of her cabin.

THE BATH WAS small and narrow, and she'd rolled

a towel to rest her head on it because the ledge was too short and square for comfort. She'd drawn up her knees nearly to her chest, but the water was hot. She was dozing after she'd bathed, when she thought she heard a creak in the room outside her door.

Maybe it was Tessa moving around. Then she heard her low whine. Either someone the dog knew was in the cabin, or someone had hurt and subdued her. If it was someone she knew, why the hell hadn't they called out?

Jamie stood and grabbed her rolled up towel. She shook it open and held it in front of her body when she stepped quietly from the tub. She'd left the light off in the outer room, so she turned off the light inside the bathroom so that her body wouldn't be framed in the opening. She reached for the doorknob and turned it slowly, and then eased open the door to peek into the room.

A large man stood in the room with his back to her. Just the light from the nightlight in the kitchen area illuminated his frame. In the dark, he looked menacing with his broad shoulders and long, muscled thighs.

If she'd been dressed, she might have

handled this differently, confronted him directly, but she'd left her clothes in a pile on the floor beside the armchair. Also, her web belt, with her holstered Glock, was on the far side of the room. She felt at a distinct disadvantage.

She picked up her brush from the counter and walked toward him as he knelt in front of Tessa. When she was a foot away, she pushed the handle of the brush against the back of his neck. "Don't move a muscle," she said, keeping her tone even.

He froze for a second. "Let me turn on a light," he said, his voice sounding muffled.

Not happening. She was naked. "How about you move toward the door. Doesn't have to be a big deal. I don't have to hurt you."

His shoulders shook, which pissed her off. Was he laughing at her?

She shoved the end of the handle harder against his skin. "Get up slowly."

He pushed up from the floor. He was as tall as Sky, and just as broad. Which pissed her off. Her fiancé was halfway around the world when she needed him most. Grasping the towel in front her and keeping the brush handle pressed against his neck, she nudged him. "Go on. Get to the door."

He took two steps then feinted right. She dropped the towel and the brush and raised both fists, prepared to fight. His next move surprised her. A foot hooked behind her knee, a hand pushed against her chest, and she was falling...

Onto the mattress of the bed. When his body settled over hers, she knew who had her pinned. She knew his weight, the feel of his muscled chest. Knew his scent.

"Sky?"

"Yes, baby?" he said, kissing her cheek.

"You're a jerk."

He skimmed his lips down the bridge of her nose then gave her a featherlight kiss on her mouth. "I know."

She moved her lips against his, rubbing harder. "Since you weren't hurt bad," she said, her tone dead even, "I expect you to make it up to me for all the worry...for breaking your goddamn phone and giving Hank that ridiculous message."

He cupped her left breast and toggled the tip with his thumb. "Sounds like I have a long list of transgressions to make up for."

"You do. Very long," she said, slipping a hand between their bodies and grasping his cock through his jeans. "I'm so glad this isn't the part of you that sustained injuries."

"Oh, it's hurting."

She smiled against his mouth. "Better get it somewhere safe and warm."

"Jesus." He braced his weight on one hand and tried to unzip his jeans, but she batted away his hand and unbuttoned and unzipped them herself. Then she slid her hands beneath the denim to cup his buttocks. She stroked a fingertip down his crack.

He hissed. "Shove them down, baby. Get my dick out."

If he felt half as desperate as she did for him to be inside her, she figured he deserved a little blue-ball punishment. She moved her hands to the front of his jeans and reached inside for his cock. She cupped his balls and slowly tightened her grip on them.

"Easy, baby."

She gave them a little shake. "You said you weren't hurt that bad. Do you know what went through my head hearing that?"

"That I wasn't hurt bad…?" he gritted out.

She shook her head. "Reaper said the same damn thing. I don't think your brains are wired like a woman's. I imagined you'd been shot and suffered a flesh would, or that an underwater mine had exploded, and you were burned or cut. That's what I imagined."

"Baby, I was shot...*at*. A round pierced the boat's armor and fragmented. I got a little shrapnel—pieces in my cheek, my shoulder, my arm. And I didn't break my phone. Another piece of shrapnel hit it dead square in the center."

"I'm so glad you set me straight," she said, fuming inside and still gripping his balls. "Now, I want you to roll over on your back."

CHAPTER 6

As soon as she released his balls, Sky rolled to his back then reached to the bedside table to find the lamp, which he turned on. He needed to see her face, in particular, her eyes, because while she sounded really angry, he was worried he'd find tears.

Sure enough, the moment she straddled his hips and leaned over him, he noted her glittering eyes. "Ah, babe." He placed his hands on her cheeks and thrust his fingers into her hair, but she didn't allow him to bring her down for a kiss.

Jamie moved her finger around the small bandages on his left cheek then over the larger ones on his shoulder and upper arm. "You'll have more scars," she said, then tightened her mouth into a straight line, likely because her lips were quivering.

"I'm fine. I'll be fine."

Her frown was ferocious. "You could have called."

"I did. I used Boomer's phone."

She shook her head. "I was outside cellphone range for a couple of days. I didn't recognize the numbers. I thought they were robocalls. I called Hank...'"

"And got my...unhelpful message...?"

She nodded, and her face screwed up. He gripped her shoulders and brought her down against his chest.

Her chest bumped against his when she sobbed. "When did you strip?"

He kissed her temple and smoothed his hands over her back. "I was planning to join you in the bathroom and surprise you, but Tessa started whining."

"I thought I had an intruder."

"Obviously. And you planned to shoot me with what?"

She let out a hoarse laugh. "My brush handle."

He smiled as she settled against him, breathing more deeply.

Jamie rubbed her cheek on his uninjured shoulder. "I'm glad you're here."

"I couldn't wait. I drove straight from Hank's. Kept in touch with Lacey. She told me she'd have a cabin for us."

"So, she knew…?"

"Don't be mad at her. She thought it would be romantic. Said she's been trying to help you with wedding plans, but you've been…resistant."

She sighed. "I don't know why I've made such a big deal about this. I'll go with whatever you want. Just don't ask me to buy a thousand-dollar gown I'll never wear again."

He chuckled. "I got some advice when I was away. Seems like we're not that far apart with what we want, Jamie. What's most important is that you're willing to wear my ring. Be my wife. The rest of it is just…details."

She lifted her head. Tears clung to her eyelashes, and she closed her eyes while he smoothed his thumbs over her lids to dry them.

"No more tears," he whispered. "No more arguing. We find this dirtbag Wakley then get hitched. The sooner the better."

She nodded her agreement and gave him a little smile. She looked lovely. Her hair was drying in gold ringlets around her shoulders. Her face was flushed with heat from her bath. Her honey-brown eyes were clear and looking lovingly at him. He basked in that look, grateful she still loved him.

He cupped her cheeks again and leaned up to kiss her. "Ride me, baby," he whispered.

Jamie settled her knees on either side of his body, and then planted her hands on the mattress beside his shoulders. She glanced down between their bodies. With a shallow movement, she lifted and pushed back on his rigid cock, circling her hips until he fit against her opening. Then she sank backwards, letting out a breathy moan as he filled her.

Lord, he'd missed this. Missed her wet heat. The feel of her soft skin.

Sky replaced his hands—thumbs on the notched bones of her hips, his fingers splayed over her ass. He pushed her down on him then waited as she rose. Sliding his feet up the mattress, he bent his knees for leverage and rocked his hips against hers.

Soon, the glides were less gentle. They slammed together, and he let go of her ass to cradle her quivering breasts. He loved looking at her this way. Loved how her features strained, loved watching the muscles of her toned thighs and belly flex as she fucked him.

When she grew breathless, he gathered her body closer and rolled, tucking her beneath him. Then he slipped his arms beneath her knees and leaned over her. With her movements restricted, he pounded against her pussy, thrusting deep and hard. Her hands fell to the pillow beneath her head, and she closed her eyes. Her head thrashed, and her breaths gusted. He was close, but he fought the urgent need to let go. He wanted her with him. Needed to watch her come apart.

He shifted his knees and gave her shorter thrusts, grinding at the end of each to rub his pubic bone and hair against her clit.

Her back arched, and her eyes widened. "Sky!"

"Yes, baby. Come now. Come with me." He pistoned his hips, moving faster, building friction until she cried out. He gave his own shout, and although his motions slowed while he spilled inside her, he didn't stop moving until she lay limply beneath him. Completely spent.

He released her legs and waited as she

stretched them out, then he turned them on their sides. Brushing away the hair sticking to her cheeks, he cradled her face. "I love you."

Sleepily, she blinked and smiled. But she didn't answer.

She slept.

THE NEXT MORNING, Sky was seated at the small table in the kitchen area of the cabin when Reaper strode through the cabin's open door. "Good to see you," he said, grinning. "See you have a few souvenirs," he said, glancing at his bandaged cheek. "Tried to tell her you weren't hurt bad."

At that moment, Jamie exited the bathroom and gave them both a scowl. "Bet Carly wouldn't have found that one bit funny."

Reaper raised his hands. "Nope. You're right. She'd have been all over my shit if I'd said something as lame-assed as you did, buddy."

"Traitor," Sky said, then chuckled.

"Hey, I said 'buddy.'" Reaper went to the sideboard and poured himself a cup of coffee. Then he took the other empty chair at the small table and winked. "Figure you've got a knee and would prefer that Jamie sit on it."

Jamie poured herself a cup and settled on Sky's knee. "So, have the guys from Kalispell arrived?"

Reaper nodded. "They're eating breakfast in Lacey and Dagger's cabin."

"Mace and Taco with them?"

"Yeah. Though I hope Tessa's feeling up to another run in the woods. We're going to split up to cover more ground, and we have sat phones Brian sent, so we can track each other's progress and won't have to rely on cellphone bars. Lacey is working with Meg Henry, Wolf's woman."

"The Flathead County deputy?"

"Yeah, she works with Fetch's office as a side gig now."

"What will she and Lacey be doing?"

"Hitting every gas station and restaurant between here and the border. They'll leave pictures of our runner and offer rewards to anyone who calls in if they give us a good lead."

"Could get expensive," Sky murmured.

"Yeah, well we can't let him get to Canada, can we?" Reaper said, holding up his cup for another sip. "We can't operate north of the border."

"With so many working this now, our cuts are going to be miniscule," Jamie said, wrinkling her nose.

"Brian can do the math. It won't be an equal split. He'll figure number of hours each hunter has spent on this clusterfuck, plus Fetch is offering a bonus to the team that brings him in."

Sky shared a smile with Jamie. "What are we waiting for?"

"For her to get off your lap?" Reaper muttered. "Or should I give you guys another twenty…alone…"

"God, I love my job," Jamie said, then fisted her hand around Sky's collar and pulled him close for a kiss.

CHAPTER 7

Two DAYS LATER, both teams were no closer to finding Wakley. However, on the previous night before nightfall finally had ended their hunt, Tessa picked up his scent.

For the two days they'd hunted, Mace with his dog Taco, Wolf, and Quincy had followed a direct path through the Flathead National Forest heading northward, the shortest route to Canada. On a hunch, because she figured Wakley had to be as tired as they were and might want to restock his provisions, Jamie and Tessa, along with Dagger, Reaper, and Sky shot an azimuth heading northwest, toward Eureka. Her hunch had been correct, because it was the exact direction Tessa's nose was leading them.

Now, they closed in on the town that sat nine miles from the Canadian border. After papering Polebridge, Lacey and Meg cut due west and canvassed every gas station and restaurant in Olney, Trego, and Fortine, before arriving in Eureka. They'd also touched base with law enforcement to make sure they kept an eye out for Wakley. Often, when it came to bail jumpers, cops didn't like the paperwork and would just as soon notify the bounty hunters where to find their skip.

After Tessa's nose hit the dirt, Reaper and Sky soon found visual evidence along the trail that their skip was getting messy, leaving evidence behind. Food wrappers, water bottles, uncovered poop.

Jamie let the guys observe that last item and make guesstimates concerning how long ago Wakley had taken his dump.

"Oh, the glamourous life we lead," Jamie murmured under her breath.

"We have to be right on his ass," Reaper said, catching up to Jamie who was following Tessa's wagging tail.

"I don't even want to know how you SEALs can guess that looking at poop. Do they have special classes in BUD/s training?"

Reaper chuckled. "We learned on the job. Follow a group of insurgents through the mountains, and you learn things."

Her sat phone rang, and she called Tessa back to her side. The call was from Lacey.

"Hey, girl, you guys nearly to Eureka?" Lacey said without a greeting.

"Should exit on the highway a couple of miles south in the next half hour. Anyone see him in Eureka?"

"Not yet, but we have flyers everywhere. Oh, and the show's cameraman turned up a couple of hours ago. He's hoping to be here for the capture."

Jamie snorted. "Warn him he may be filming a bunch of sad faces if we don't find Wakley soon. He's within spitting distance of Canada."

"He said he'd be just as happy watching you guys hike up to the border station and look all forlorn. Said every hunt can't end on a good note or viewers will think we're a scripted reality show."

"Good to know he sees a fucking silver lining."

Lacey laughed. "Good to know you're still in

bubbly mood, you know, now that you and Sky are sharing a sleeping bag."

"We are not. Ever have sex in the summer in the woods? Too many damn mosquitoes."

Lacey cleared her throat. "Thought you might want to know things could get trickier than usual once you get to Eureka."

Jamie looked skyward. Would they ever catch a break? "Oh, God. What now?"

"The town's having some summer event. An ATV convention, it looks like. Free outdoor barbecue. A mud race…"

Now, that didn't sound so bad. "Sounds like something a man who's been chowing down on protein bars might not be able to resist."

"I'll send Meg with the vehicle to pick you up on the highway. Send your coordinates when you get to the road. I'll be at the barbecue next to the river."

Jamie ended the call and headed back to the men waiting for her. "Meg Henry's picking us up on the highway. Looks like we're going to a barbecue."

Less than half an hour later, Jamie sat in front of the SUV with Meg, after shedding her rain gear and rolling it up. A sudden downpour had struck the moment she'd gotten off the phone with Lacey.

After rolling up her rain poncho and stowing it in her pack, she'd called shotgun but moved her seat as far forward as she could to make room for Reaper's "delicate stems".

"So," Jamie said, looking at the redhead next to her. "How are you liking bounty hunting?"

Meg laughed. "The sheriff asks me that all the time. I think he's worried I'll go over to the dark side." She shot Jamie a glance. "I like it fine, though. Especially when I can work with Wolf. If I didn't use my downtime hunting, we'd really find it hard to spend time together. I never realized how busy you guys were until I hired on. Now, I don't know how you manage to keep sane with a production crew following you around, too.

Jamie shook her head. "Sometimes, I regret signing the contract, but the checks sure are nice."

"I bet," Meg said smiling. "Looks like our office is going to get some exposure on your television show today."

Jamie noted that she wrinkled her nose. "Will that be a problem?"

"Just so long as your fans don't go and give us nicknames like 'Bounty Hunter Barbie.'"

Jamie grinned. "Lacey's all into that. Plays it up."

"She's something. Must be a lot of fun to work with."

"She makes life interesting. That's for sure."

The women laughed. Jamie glanced back at Dagger to make sure he was okay with them talking about his woman, but he shrugged and gave her a wink.

They passed through the long strip of road that was Eureka's main street then followed the signs to the barbecue taking place along the banks of the Tobacco River. When they arrived at a grassy parking lot, Meg found a spot far from the entrance of the event. Two more dark SUVs were parked there. The doors opened. More hunters emerged.

Jamie shook her head. She hadn't seen this many MBH hunters in one place...well, ever. The biggest surprise was seeing Fetch among the mix. She walked up to him and reached out her hand to shake, but he ignored her hand and gave her a hug.

"Long time no see," he said when he let her

go. "And what's this about you fighting with Sky over wedding plans?"

Jamie's eyes widened, and she shot a glare at Reaper.

Reaper glanced away, whistling.

She'd have a little talk with him later. Maybe put that photo of him hugging Carlito on the website for the entire world to see.

She glanced around the group. Yeah, no way Wakley would mistake them for locals out to enjoy a barbecue. "Fetch, is every hunter in MBH here today?"

"Not quite, as you well know. You still have three working in Glacier. But there's not a more important skip to catch than our friend Wakley. He's not afraid to use a weapon. He'll escalate if he's left free."

Jamie nodded, knowing what he said was true. Still, it seemed like overkill having so many hunters dedicated to this takedown. But she wasn't the big boss...

She turned to address the group. "I'm thinking we should enter a few at a time," she said. "And go fully armed, and with our vests. This is Montana. Folks around here won't blink. But if they do, maybe they'll see our badges and decide to stay clear of us. There's no way of knowing if Wakley's even here. For all we know, he's already stolen supplies and is back out in the woods. By nightfall, he could easily be across the border. However, if he is here, we want a clean takedown." She pointed to the cameraman, who already held his camera on his shoulder filming. "And ignore the fact he's here. Keep your head in the game. Melvin Wakley is a violent man. I don't want anyone hurt, especially not any of the town folk here to have a good time. Any questions?"

When no one answered, she said, "Let's head out. We have a dipshit to arrest."

SKY LOVED WATCHING Jamie take charge of their merry band of hunters. Seeing her so confident and knowing every man there respected her, made him feel proud he was the guy who got to take her home.

The hunters made an intimidating sight as they moved through the crowd, gazes scanning the vendors' stalls and rows of banquet tables.

Sky kept his gaze scanning as he walked, but his boots made annoying sucking sounds. Where there wasn't wet grass, there was slick, gooey mud.

Ahead of him, Jamie had Tessa on a lead, keeping her close to her side. Suddenly, Tessa's body stiffened. Her nose lifted, scenting the air. She gave a sharp bark then strained against her leash.

Jamie released some leash and hurried forward, letting the dog dart through the crowd, making her way toward the row of four-wheelers lined up on display, salesmen hovering over customers. Beyond the line of ATVs was a dirt track, where locals drove their four-wheelers around a muddy obstacle course, their tires leaving deep grooves in the muck.

Tessa ran straight toward the track, but Jamie pulled her lead near the end of the line of shiny new ATVs. Sky stopped beside her, and they watched as a young man in a helmet ran toward them.

"Hey!" the teenager said, as came closer. He pointed toward a red ATV nearing the end of the track. "That guy pulled me off my ATV. He has a gun!"

Jamie turned to a salesman and raised her badge. "These vehicles have gas?" she asked.

He gave her a nod and tossed her a set of keys. "Take that one," he said, pointing toward one painted in a green and black camouflage pattern.

"Got another?" Sky asked. Keys flew, and the salesman pointed toward another rugged-looking vehicle.

More hunters appeared, and Jamie tossed Tessa's leash to Lacey. "Keep her off the track. Wakley's making a run for it."

They both mounted, started the ignitions, and gunned their engines. Sky kept behind Jamie as she leaned forward and headed in a straight line toward Wakley, who was heading toward the forest on the far side of the clearing.

Wakley had the lead but didn't have the fastest ride. Jamie was on his tail before he hit the forest line.

Then they were racing around trees, through thickets, engines roaring.

Wakley made the mistake of glancing back at his pursuers. When he turned forward again, he was aimed at a tree. He steered hard to the right, and the wheels on that side left the ground. He rolled the ATV, which landed upside down with him several feet away. He quickly pushed up to his feet and ran.

They chased him through the forest, but he soon slowed, tripping over vines and smacking against tree trunks. They let him tire, waiting for the moment he'd stop and make his stand.

When he slid behind a tree, Sky didn't have time to give a shout. He saw the barrel of a handgun appear from around the tree and gunned his engine, circling to the left while Jamie went right. He kicked off the vehicle, letting it roll past Wakley while he took cover, drew his weapon, and shot high and into the tree. A warning.

Jamie stopped her vehicle and slid behind another tree. They shared glances. He smiled. She scowled. Then she tilted her head toward Wakley, telling him silently to wait for his opening.

"Melvin," she shouted. "We have agents closing in all around you. You have nowhere left to run. Do yourself a favor. End it now. Throw down your gun and come out with your hands up."

His barrel disappeared from the left side of the tree. Sky knew he was taking aim at Jamie.

He moved stealthily through the brush, while she continued to banter.

"You're going to spend some time in jail, but you'll want a chance at freedom, someday. Shooting us won't help you. You'll spend the rest of your life in jail."

"I know who you are," Wakley shouted. "You're those hunters on the TV. Hollywood hunters. You got a film crew out here?"

"We do," she said. "Want to be famous?"

"I can be real famous if I take you down."

Sky made his way behind Wakley. He was almost there.

"That's not the kind of fame you want to chase, Melvin," Jamie said.

"Don't need another woman tellin' me what I should want, you mouthy bitch."

Sky took another step. A twig snapped beneath his boot.

Wakley jerked around, and Sky knew he had only a second as the man turned his weapon and pointed it at his chest. They both fired.

Blood blossomed on Wakley's right shoulder, and his gun fell out of his hand. Sky dropped to his knees, with his breath knocked out of him.

Jamie ran forward, making it to Wakley and

kicking away his weapon before turning to Sky. "You hit?"

"Kevlar," he gritted out, because it hurt like hell, and he felt like he'd been stomped on by a horse. "Not hurt bad... Be okay."

CHAPTER 8

SUDDENLY, they were surrounded by more hunters, moving in to secure Wakley. They got him to his feet and led him away. Sky barely noticed because he was trying to remember how to breathe.

Jamie moved toward him and went down on her knees beside him. She began pulling at the Velcro fastenings on his vest, pushed the vest off his shoulders, then went to work shoving up his T-shirt. Her hands smoothed over the huge red welt on his ribs, and then she pressed on it.

"Fuck," he gritted out.

"You might have cracked a rib or two," she said, her eyebrows lowered.

"I didn't. I'm just bruised. I'm fine."

"We'll need to get you to the hospital to have the doctors take some x-rays."

"They'll have to wait."

She locked her gaze with his and scowled. "The others can handle getting him to jail."

"That's not what I'm talking about." He shook his head. "Just…let me get up." When he was on his feet, she crossed her arms over her chest, and her expression turned mulish. Sky had to bite back a grin.

Reaper and Dagger were rocking his ATV and easily turned it over. Sky walked toward them and gave them a nod. "Better get back. Make sure Brian's here," he said under his breath.

Reaper grinned. "Don't make me come look for you."

Sky noted the cameraman still hanging back. He gave him a faint nod then turned to Jamie, making sure the cameraman had a view of both of their profiles.

"You're up to something. What's going on?" Jamie asked.

He cleared his throat and crossed his arms over his chest, mimicking her stance. "Staking my claim. Making damn sure you don't have any wiggle room left."

Her eyebrows shot upward. "You think I need wiggle room? Wait..." She tilted her head. "Are you talking about the wedding? I told you last night I'd do whatever you want. I'm through fighting about...details."

He reached for her hands and held them. "Then let's make it today. Now."

She blinked and leaned away, her eyes narrowing as she studied his face. Then she drew a deep breath. "Ah, I get it. That's why Fetch is here. And that huge-ass crew of hunters."

Sky wrinkled his nose. "The Kalispell guys are taking Wakley in, because we have some business to conduct."

Her lips thinned, but then the corners twitched. "I don't have a dress."

"No, you don't. Do you need one?"

She shook her head. "You arrange this with Lacey?"

He smiled. "Just tell me you'll do it. Honor your promise to go along with whatever I want."

She grimaced, but her cheeks were flushed a lovely rose. So, there was a smudge or two of mud on her face. She'd be a radiant bride.

Jamie tilted up her chin. "Guess we better hurry back then before I change my mind."

He tugged her hands, and she fell against him. As they kissed, he drew the rubber band from the bottom of her braid and sifted through her hair, loosening it. The easier for Lacey to get a brush through the tangles.

When they broke apart, she gave him a coy glance from beneath her lashes. "Race you!" Then she ran to her four-wheeler.

Smiling, he followed her all the way back to the gathering beside the river.

So, she didn't get married in her muddy clothes. While Jamie had been traipsing through the woods, Lacey had headed back to Sky and Jamie's house with instructions concerning what to bring—a clean pair of well-polished cowboy boots, freshly washed Levis, and a powder-blue chambray shirt with tiny pink flowers. Lacey made quick work of fashioning a braided crown atop Jamie's head with sprigs of baby's breath woven in. She carried a small wildflower bouquet.

She'd never felt prettier than when she stood in front of Sky with his stormy, blue-gray eyes looking down at her. And he looked so handsome, she knew all the women in the crowd around them were sighing. Dark hair, chiseled features, those stunning blue eyes, a well-built frame...

Being Jamie, she still had some questions. She glanced to the side at Reaper, who still wore his black Kevlar vest, but who had washed his face and hands. It appeared that he'd be officiating this hastily arranged wedding. "Is this even going to be legal?" she asked him.

Reaper gave her a wink. "I got my license over the internet last night in the cabin." He reached into a pocket and pulled out a printout that was wet around the folds, but which proclaimed him to be a minister in the Universal Life Church and eligible to perform weddings.

"You did that for me?"

Reaper shrugged and a blush stole across his rugged features. "Someone had to do it."

"And I brought the license for him to sign," Sky said. "No more excuses."

She narrowed her eyes. "Wasn't making one. Just wanted to be sure this thing will stick."

The crowd around them laughed. They were on a small dais with all the attendees standing on the wet grass. Fetch had walked her up the "aisle" formed in the crowd of her friends from MBH and the locals who'd stuck around to be a part of the TV moment the cameraman had really been recruited to capture.

With Brian, Fetch, and Tessa standing right behind her, she felt at peace and warmed by the thoughtfulness of her soon-to-be husband and friends. This was the wedding she hadn't been able to articulate that she wanted.

"By the way," Fetch said behind her. "You two earned the special bonus. I'm sending you to Hawaii."

Reaper cleared his throat. "So, if no one has any objections, let's get these two hitched!"

JAMIE SURFACED a few feet from Sky and waved at him. She moved the mouthpiece of her snorkel to the side and pointed downward. "Turtle!" she said, excitement in her voice. They'd snorkeled off the beach in front of their hotel in Oahu every day without having sighted a single turtle. Seeing one had been their goal since they'd arrived six days ago.

Their honeymoon had passed in a haze of sex, lavish room service dinners, more sex, and daily swims to see the underwater wildlife around the coral reef. Neither had wanted to do the usual touristy things, other than attend a luau, which they'd crossed off their list on day three, both taking hula lessons and grimacing over the taste of the traditional Hawaiian dish of poi. Mostly, they'd wanted to spend time with each other, holding each other, making love and plans for their future.

He followed her down to the reef they'd been exploring, and he saw the large oval shell of a turtle as it gracefully swam toward deeper water. Jamie stayed several feet above it, not interfering with it or trying to touch it, just watching for as long as her breath held out. Then she kicked her flippers toward the surface.

They made their way to the beach and flopped down on the blanket they'd laid in the sand. She turned her head toward him. "This has been really nice."

"But?"

She arched a brow. "Does there have to be one?"

"I heard it in your voice," he said, his tone dry.

"You know me so well." She leaned toward

him and kissed him. "But...I can't wait to get back and see what's been happening at work."

Sky chuckled. "You don't think Reaper has it all handled?"

Jamie snorted. "Reaper needs a keeper."

"Which means you. Should I be jealous?"

"Of course not. You're the person with whom I want to spend every day and night for the rest of my life. But Reaper..." she shook her head, "after Tessa, he's my best friend."

Sky nodded solemnly. "We really do have the best life, don't we?"

"Yes, friends who've always got our backs, a beautiful home with a view of the mountains, and each other."

"Have you thought any more about that other thing on our To Do list?"

She placed her palms on either side of his face. "Sky, baby, I stopped taking the pill a month ago."

He drew a deep breath. "You did?"

"Uh huh. Figured if I got pregnant, neither of us would have any more excuses left. We'd have to get married right away."

"Do you think...?"

She reached for his hand then rolled over his

body. "Making a baby in Hawaii would be the icing on the wedding cake we never had."

They kissed, and he flirted his hands along the sides of her breasts. "Guess I shouldn't start something we can't finish here," he muttered.

"Then we best get moving now, because *that's* going to be hard to hide beneath a towel," she said, rubbing against his growing erection.

"You did that on purpose," he growled as she rolled away and stood.

She tossed a beach towel at him.

He looped it around his hips, but she was right. There was no hiding what was tenting the front. Bending, he swiped up the blanket, not allowing her to fold it, and bundled it in front of his waist.

Then they ran toward their hotel, barefoot and laughing.

They didn't notice the cellphones recording their publicly private moment, but soon the world would know their love wasn't something scripted. It was true.

IF YOU LOVED **Big Sky Wedding,** *you might want*

to try **New Orleans Nights**, *which features another very sexy SEAL. Enjoy the bonus story I'm including,* "Quincy Down Under", *which is the prequel to* **Quincy: A Montana Bounty Hunters Story.**

QUINCY DOWN UNDER

Delilah Devlin

QUINCY
Down Under

MONTANA BOUNTY HUNTERS

NEW YORK TIMES BESTSELLING AUTHOR

DELILAH DEVLIN

QUINCY DOWN UNDER

"Looks like a damn hickey," the elderly beauty operator said in her raspy voice as she set the straightening wand in its metal stand.

Tamara Adams rose from the seat at Miss Gracie's station and leaned closer toward the marquee lights. Yup, the tender mark on her neck did indeed look like a love bite. She touched her finger to the burn and hissed.

"A little aloe vera will fix you right up," Miss Gracie said and rummaged through a drawer to pick up a tube that looked to be twenty years old and squeezed of all its precious cream.

Tamara bit back a grimace and waved the woman away. "Thank you so much for straightening the back of my hair, but I'll take care of the burn. You have a dinner at the senior center. Don't want to be late," she sang.

Miss Gracie's eyebrows shot halfway up her forehead. "Thanks for reminding me." She quickly retrieved her purse from her bottom drawer and headed toward the door leading out of the beauty shop.

The older woman glanced down at the cinder block holding the door open then gave Tamara a pointed stare. Tamara waved her hand in acknowledgement of the issue she still hadn't addressed, and then held her breath as the woman slowly climbed the steep steps. Miss Gracie disappeared into the sunlight that filtered down the metal staircase—the only natural lighting in Tamara's tiny shop.

When she was alone, Tamara moved toward her own station, her Sketchers sticking to the misting of hairspray that always surrounded Miss Gracie's chair, making a sound reminiscent of Squidward's tentacles.

She opened her own drawer, pulled out a tube of concealer, then did her best to mask the nasty red burn. So, maybe she should have treated it with antibiotic cream first, but she planned to hit Slim 'n' Shorty's for a drink as soon as she finished cleaning up and counting her earnings for the day.

Tamara snorted. Wouldn't take a minute to empty her cash drawer. Miss Gracie's elderly clients, the ones who could make it down the steep steps, had been the only customers that day.

Staring into her well-lit mirror, Tamara didn't get it. She was a walking advertisement for her skills. Her messy wavy, chin-length bob was all the rage in Hollywood. The platinum color with the lone rose-pink streak was flawless.

But she knew the problem was the location of her shop, and the fact she needed more noticeable signage for customers to even find it. Again, she snorted.

Hell, a billboard wouldn't be enough to convince women to make the trek down into her doomsday-bunker-turned-hair-salon.

Footsteps sounded on the metal staircase, and she whirled, excited that she'd have at least one paying customer this day. However, the huge man descending the steps wiped her smile away.

There was something about him that told her he was trouble. The hairs on the back of her neck prickled. She'd have to remember to take a razor to them later.

She pasted on a polite expression. "Hello, sir. Can I help you?"

The man's dark beady eyes glanced around her small shop. Sure, it was economy-sized, with just two stations and a very small sitting area.

His aroma hit her before she could clearly see his face. He smelled musty, like he'd worn the same clothes for at least a week, and she wondered if he understood the concept of deodorant.

She gave him a tight smile as he drew closer, reminding herself she had a lighter and a can of hairspray close by. "Would you like a shave or a haircut?" He was sorely in need of both. His long beard looked matted like a dog's after a week in the woods, and his stringy hair nearly met his shoulders.

He walked toward her chair and eyed it.

"It's old, but it won't collapse," she murmured then held up her hands. "Not that I'm saying you're fat or anything." Her face suffused with heat. "It's sturdier than it looks."

He sat, which brought him down to eyelevel with her. The pockmarks on his cheeks and the dark, deep-set eyes made him look even more sinister.

"Shave the beard, and I need a cut," he said, "and I need to change the color."

She blinked. Maybe he'd realized he'd never get a date unless he made an effort with his appearance. Bathing regularly would also greatly increase his odds. "I can help with that. Do you have anything in particular in mind?"

His mouth curved, but the smile didn't lessen her nervousness, so she began to set out the implements of her trade and bent to pull a fresh cape from the stack on the shelf beside her station.

She started with his beard, telling herself not to rush, because the last thing she wanted to do was nick him. She trimmed away the excess hair then slathered on shaving cream. When she picked up her straight razor, he reached out and gripped her wrist. Alarmed, she shot him wide-eyed glance. "It gives the closest shave," she said, and gave him another inane smile. "I'm going to lean your chair back so I can reach you." When he let go of her wrist, she lowered his chair and leaned it backward.

His gaze drilled into her, and she read the silent warning in his narrowed eyes.

After taking a deep breath to still the tremor in her hands, she shaved him then patted his pink cheeks with an aftershave. The scent helped to mask his odor, and she felt a little more confident as she returned him to an upright position and turned the chair to face her mirror. She met his gaze in the glass. "Now for the cut. Do you want it short?"

He nodded.

"And you mentioned color," she said, eyeing his dirty brown hair. "Would you like the tips highlighted?"

"Bleach it all."

"Oh." Her eyebrows rose, because she couldn't imagine blond hair against his swarthy complexion. "Are you sure?"

"Just do it."

She swallowed. "I'll give you a cut first. Then I'll bleach your hair."

When he didn't object, she picked up her scissors and began snipping away his lanky locks. She glanced at the clock. It was nearly five. She wasn't going to have time to change before she headed to the bar. She'd hoped to be there early to get a seat close to Mason Jernigan's usual table. She hadn't had a date in forever and hoped to catch his eye. While she wasn't looking for love, she did hope for a hookup. A girl needed a little attention to keep her confidence up. She'd recently turned thirty and had been a little depressed over the fact her life plan wasn't shaping up the way she'd thought it would when she'd been younger.

After she trimmed away the bulk of his hair, she used her electric razor to fade the sides. She left the top spiky, because she figured the height would make his face look less round. At last, she pulled out the products she needed and quickly mixed the bleach in a bowl.

Forty-five minutes later, she used wax to spike up his newly washed hair and watched his expression in the mirror. She couldn't tell if he was pleased or not, but she wasn't counting on a fat tip from her surly customer. "All done," she said and swept away the cape. "Since you're the last customer of the day, I'll cut you a break. It's just sixty-five dollars."

He laughed as he pushed up from his seat.

She drew a deep breath and stepped back, once again wary of the menace in his demeanor. "I can take cash, check, or credit card. I have the Square…"

Only, he was already moving toward the door.

"If you're not happy, I'll knock the price down to fifty," she called after him.

He never glanced back, and she chewed on her lip, trying to tamp down a sudden flare of anger. She'd spent an hour and a half on the bastard and used her expensive products. She deserved to be paid.

At the stand beside the door, he picked up the telephone. Her land line—the only phone that worked in the bunker because the thick metal ceiling prevented cellphone signals from coming through.

She held her breath as he drew back his arm and pulled the cord out of the wall. "Son of a bitch," she muttered under her breath, but she didn't move toward him. Her gaze cut to the small bathroom door in the corner. If she had to, she'd barricade herself inside.

Apparently, he wasn't planning to attack her. He paused and glanced down at the cinderblock doorstop she'd placed to keep the door open... because the door latch locked from the outside...

He kicked it away, and she heard his low, cruel laughter as he slammed the door closed.

QUINCY JAMES DROVE SLOWLY past the small single-story house, his gaze flicking over the home and the neat yard, and then zeroing in on the gold Buick parked in the driveway with a license plate number that matched his target's to a T. He passed the house and parked in front of one farther down with an empty driveway, hoping there'd be no one home to make any noise about him leaving his truck in front of their yard.

He grabbed his cellphone from the cupholder and hit the auto-dial for the office.

"Montana Bounty Hunt—wait, that you, Quincy?" Brian Cobb, the agency's office manager said.

"Yeah, Bri. Guess his cousin wasn't lying about his intentions. I found Clay Horner's Buick. Took your advice and hit the beauty shops in Amity, though I'm not sure the address was right for this one... But it's his car. Plate matches."

"Okay, you hold tight. Reaper and Hook are still in Whitefish."

Quincy's eyes narrowed. He might be new to the Montana Bounty Hunters, but he'd been working this gig for seven years. Solo. He wasn't waiting a damn hour for reinforcements to arrive. For the hundredth time, he wondered why the hell he'd agreed to sign on with the agency. He liked working alone and liked even better keeping all the money he earned—not splitting it with team members.

Horner's bounty would bring in a cool ten grand. To his mind, a three-way split was only a good thing when it had something to do with gymnastic twins.

Still, he'd seen the big ticket takedowns the agency had been making lately, so when he'd been approached by Reaper, he'd said he'd give it six months to see how things worked out.

"You're not much of a team player, are you?" Reaper had asked over their third round of beers.

Quincy grunted. "I quit being a team player when I left the Army."

Reaper's mouth stretched into a grin. "My

wife's ex-Army. The man who owns the agency is ex-Army. You might find it easier than you think being a part of this team."

Well, he'd only been an MBH hunter for a couple of weeks, so he'd been surprised when Reaper had sent him on his own to Amity to look for leads. He'd been riding along with Hook since he'd hired on. Maybe they'd finally realized he knew his shit when they'd beat the bushes for Roddy Wainwright last weekend out in Glacier. Quincy had been the one to find him. When the rest of the team arrived after he'd radioed, he'd been drinking coffee from the metal coffee can Roddy had rigged over his fire, casually shooting the breeze with the grizzly poacher, who was cuffed, but otherwise appeared none the worse for wear.

Quincy let himself out of out of his truck. He passed the mailbox. It matched the address he'd pulled off the internet when he'd Googled "beauty and barber shops in Amity." However, it wasn't until he snuck around the house, peering into windows without seeing a soul, that he happened upon a small sign with an arrow pointing toward "Curl Up & Dye." The scissors that substituted for the ampersand looked as though a child had drawn them.

Around the back of the house, he found a flagstone pathway leading to a metal staircase that descended into the ground. He drew his weapon and slowly crept down to the closed metal door, stepping over a cinder block before reaching out to pull on the door handle.

The door creaked open, and he peered inside. The interior of the shop was darker than outside, so he moved even slower, letting his eyes adjust to the dimness inside. Behind him, he heard the door creak as it slowly swung closed.

It was then he heard a click and fire shot toward him. He stumbled backward, tripping over something beside the door and landing on his ass.

Blinded, he raised his gun. "What the fuck?"

"Drop the gun or I'll fry your ass!" came a garbled voice. Another click sounded, and more flame shot toward him.

This time, heat curled the hairs on his forearm. "All right," he said, cussing under his breath. He slowly laid his gun on the cool concrete floor.

"Now, get up," the voice said, this time more

clearly. And definitely a woman's voice. "Head toward the lighted mirror."

He raised his hands and strode toward the bright lights. "Lady, I'm not looking for trouble."

"And all the other asshole wanted was a haircut," she said, bitterness in her tone. "You can take a seat."

He sat and glanced into the glass to find a very pretty woman wielding a can of hairspray. He almost smiled, but he was intrigued. "I'm a bounty hunter. Was that other asshole a big guy with a beard?"

Her eyebrows lowered. "You're a big guy with a beard. Show me your badge. For all I know, he sent you to get a cut and bleach, too. He owes me sixty-five bucks."

He began to lower his hands, but she quickly raised her spray can higher. "Badge is on my belt, ma'am," he ground out.

"Just no funny moves. Better yet…" she said, reaching sideways and pulling what looked like clothesline cord from a shelf. "Put your hands behind you."

Quincy conceded it might have been smarter to wait for that backup. "You don't have to tie my hands. I swear I'm a bounty hunter. Just call Montana Bounty Hunters in Bear Lodge—"

"Can't call. The asshole tore out my land line."

"Don't you have a cellphone?"

"Yeah, smart ass, but you can't get a signal through a metal roof and six feet of dirt."

He put his hands behind him and let her wind the cord around and around his wrists. When she'd finished tying him, he surreptitiously pulled against his restraints and realized the woman knew her knots. "Okay, now will you go outside and make that call? I'm not going anywhere."

In the mirror, he watched as her lower lip began to tremble.

She spun away. "Can't call. We're stuck here. The door locks from the outside."

Quincy blinked. *No fucking way.* Reaper and Hook would bust their guts laughing when they arrived.

"We'll be here until tomorrow morning when Miss Gracie comes to work."

He opened his mouth to reassure her they'd be rescued soon, but instead, pursed his lips. He didn't know her. Maybe she was involved with

Clay Horner. "The asshole you mentioned before…"

She sniffed and raised her free hand, likely to wipe away a tear or two, then turned to meet his gaze in the glass. "He came in just before closing. Said he wanted a shave and cut. Then he asked me to bleach his hair."

Quincy nodded. "He give you a name?"

She shook her head. "I was too nervous to ask for one." She sniffed, and her mouth settled into a straight line. "He was big, with a scraggly beard nearly to his chest and shoulder-length hair. And he had small beady eyes, like a pig's."

Quincy let out a deep breath and settled back in his chair. "That's Horner, all right. You're lucky all he wanted was a cut. He's wanted for armed robbery."

"Probably knew I hardly have a dime," she said, the corners of her mouth drooping. "He stiffed me for the bill then locked me inside."

"Look," he said, "I have a badge. It's on my belt."

Her gaze narrowed, but she moved closer.

Once she was within reach of the bright lights from the multitude of bulbs surrounding the mirror, Quincy's eyes widened before he blinked and recovered himself. He'd thought her pretty before, but her soft-looking wavy hair with its cotton-candy pink streak made him wish his hands were free to touch it. Her skin was pale, her eyes an unusual blue-gray, framed by dark lashes. Her brows were dark, but they only heightened the appeal of her pretty eyes. Her mouth was a soft, pale pink, with a very full lower lip.

When she bent nearer and reached for his belt, he kept his expression neutral although he fought a smile, spread his legs, and raised his hips so he could lean back a bit to help her out. Her fingers fumbled with the clip-on, but eventually she freed it—after tugging enough to get something a little farther south excited over her small jerking motions.

She didn't say a word as her gaze lowered to the bulge in his pants, but her breath caught.

Quincy wished he had a glib tongue, but he never said the right things to women. He didn't have a clue what he ought to say to ease this awkward moment, but he tried anyway. "It's your mouth," he muttered. "And…your hair. And…you know, you have really pretty eyes." He nearly groaned at how ridiculous he sounded, but he had a great excuse. All the blood had rushed south to fill his cock, leaving his brain defenseless.

"You think I'm pretty?" she asked, and her face crumpled again.

"Look, don't cry. It's going to be okay. You can even keep me tied up. I'm no threat. And yeah, you're...pretty." Although pretty didn't begin to cover it. Everything about her blew him away. She looked like an extra-curvy Barbie doll with lush tits, a nice inward curve at her waist, and an ass that would more than fill his big palms. He winced because now his cock pushed harder against stiff denim.

"Did I tie the rope too tight?"

"No," he said, grimacing. "But I can't, um, adjust myself."

"Adjust...?" She glanced down at the front of his pants. "Sorry."

"Don't be. It's just been a while. And being like this, with you...well..."

"I see." She chewed her lower lip. "I can't untie you. I don't really know you..."

He closed his eyes. "Maybe if I don't look at you...things...will ease."

She made a little noise, and he peeked up at

her. After setting down the hairspray can and lighter, she moved in front of him, and her hands reached out…

His breath hitched as she reached for his belt and unbuckled it. He sucked in a deeper breath when she unbuttoned his jeans. The easing of the constriction made him groan. He slowly opened his eyes. "Thanks."

"That help?"

"A little." Would she be moved to do more if she thought he was still in pain? At that moment, he hoped like hell Reaper and Hook took their sweet time getting there.

Again, her teeth worried her bottom lip.

"What's your name?" he asked, his voice going deeper.

"Tamara. Tamara Adams."

"I'm Quincy James. You can check that out. Wallet's in my right front pocket." For once, his non-glib tongue worked.

Pink rose in her cheeks, but she nodded and moved to his side before sliding her slim hand inside his pocket. Her fingers spread wide, wider than necessary. Fingers pushed against the side of his dick.

His chest rose. "Easy now," he whispered.

"Got it," she said, and slid his wallet free.

"No, you didn't," he muttered.

In the mirror, he saw the way her lips curved at the corners as she flipped open the wallet. "Quincy James. And you live in Bear Lodge. You're a couple of months younger than I am." Her gaze went to his profile. "Picture doesn't do you justice."

His mouth twitched, but he held back a smile.

She freed his driver's license and moved in front of him again. Then she held it up. "Hmmm. Hazel eyes." She leaned toward him. "They look pretty green to me. Brown hair…" Her gaze went from his hair, which was in need of a trim, to his beard. She thrust her fingers into his beard and cupped his jaw. "Not hiding a weak chin…"

He narrowed his eyes, which elicited a grin from her. When her mouth stretched, he drew a shaky breath. "Damn, I thought you were pretty before."

The blonde in front of him tilted her head. "Are you flirting with me?"

"Don't know how." Which had been the truth until she'd tied him to the chair.

Her gaze flickered downward.

His followed. "I'm feeling a little desperate

now." The truth. "I'm a little twisted in there." A lie. "If I get any harder, blood flow might be restricted." A definite possibility if she kept chewing on her lip the way she was now.

"Well, I don't want to maim you for life," she muttered, sounding a little breathless.

His heartbeat kicked up a notch. Was she considering doing something about his predicament? Sweet Jesus, he hoped so.

"You married?" she said, aiming a sharp glance at his face.

"Nope. Never."

"Because you don't like commitment?" she asked, narrowing her eyes.

"No. Because I'm not good at chatting up women. You all make me nervous."

"Seriously?" She huffed a breath. "You're not a bad-looking man."

He arched an eyebrow.

She rolled her eyes. "Okay, so you're...attractive—if a girl was into a rugged kind of guy."

"You know anyone like that? Maybe you can give me her number," he growled.

"No girlfriend?"

He met her gaze and held still. "I don't have anyone—not a wife, not a girlfriend, not a friendly hookup. And I haven't fucked anyone in months."

Her blush deepened. "Really? Me, too!" And then she seemed to catch herself and whirled away.

"Now, I have a hard time believing that," he said softly. "Girl as pretty as you are, with a body any man would be grateful to pin to a bed..." So, maybe he'd taken that a little too far.

Only, she was peeking at him over her shoulder, and she didn't look mad or disgusted. No, her gaze was steady as it swept his face then moved down to his crotch again.

Quincy began to think that, just maybe, he'd managed to say the right thing for once. "It's okay if you want to slap my face."

When she turned and walked back to him, her hips swayed like a pendulum, entrancing him. "Something needs slapped," she said, her voice huskier than before.

"I'm at your mercy, ma'am."

She raised a finger and touched his nose then traced a path downward to his lips. "Mercy... mercy...me," she whispered, leaning closer so that her sweet breath gusted against his face. "I should free him, so he isn't damaged. That would be a cryin' shame."

Quincy didn't mind that she was more worried about his cock than him. He'd never seen or heard anything sexier in all his days as her pouty mouth talking about his dick that way. "I'm not cryin', but I might howl," he whispered back.

A grin spread across her mouth.

"That a little cheesy?" he asked, wrinkling his nose but not worried because she was moving her hands over his shirt, slowly shaping his shoulders, then moving them lower.

"Have to make sure you're not packing anything under your clothes…"

He held back a quip, not wanting to halt her pat down. The way she smoothed her palms over his ribs and belly made his muscles jump.

When she reached his hips, he blurted, "Do you need me to rise up?"

"Would kind of defeat the purpose if you didn't," she drawled.

His gaze locked with hers. She didn't break eye contact to glance down as he lifted and she gripped his waistband. With a couple of hard shoves, she pushed his pants, along with his briefs, to the tops of his thighs.

His cock thrust up from his groin, jerking with his heartbeats.

"That better?" she asked then licked her lips.

He gave a muffled moan. "Better? Jesus, girl."

She laughed, and the sound did things to his skin—causing goosebumps to rise because he liked it so much.

"Oh my," she said, her gaze locked on his dick. "Don't think I've seen one so…"

"Big?"

She blinked and raised her face. Her blush intensified. "Yeah. And the shape…"

He frowned.

Again, she blinked. "What I mean… It's not bad…" She drew a deep breath and reached out a fingertip to trace the cap. "The top…it's shaped like a doorknob. Kind of."

He pressed his lips together to hold back a bark of laughter. Or maybe a groan, because she had just touched his dick. "Does it worry you?"

"Why should I be worried?" she asked, lifting her chin. "All I did was free it…from constriction."

"Uh huh."

She cleared her throat, and her glance slid away. "A girl might be a little...concerned."

"It'll fit, Tamara," he said softly, holding his breath, because he didn't want her to skitter away and leave him like this.

THE FIT WASN'T her worry. Being stretched so deliciously that any other man would fall short— or rather, thin—in comparison, was a very real concern. She could already imagine how he'd feel inside her. The stretch, the burn. *The bliss.*

All the while she'd teased him, watching him get harder and harder, smiling inwardly over his clumsy responses, she'd grown aroused, too.

She, Tamara Adams, had a man tied to her chair with his dick standing between his legs. She couldn't remember the name of the man she'd thought she'd try to seduce that night. His face was forgotten. Quincy James threw shade all over him.

And Quincy appeared willing to let her do anything she wanted. He thought she was pretty. He'd stuttered over his description of what he found attractive about her, and every time he'd named a feature, his gaze had lingered. He wasn't lying. His dick confirmed the truth. He wanted her.

So...*why not?*

Would she ever have another chance to do something this decadent? And it wasn't like he lived in Amity. She didn't have to worry about running into him when she was at the grocery store and dying of embarrassment. No, she could do this, and after they were rescued, she could kiss him goodbye. Because she knew she couldn't hold the interest of someone like him. She was hairdresser who worked out of her dad's old bunker. He was a man with a dangerous profession, who likely traveled a lot and did exciting things all the time. What would he want with her?

Though a disappointing thought, it also emboldened her. She glanced at the chair. It might be a problem. The arms would only give her a very narrow space to straddle him. Her gaze went to the old sofa with its duct-taped seams. Her father had placed it in the bunker twenty years ago. And then he'd used the bunker as his mancave to escape and dream about foreign invaders.

Not for the first time, she knew he was probably rolling in his grave because of what she'd done with his special place.

Well, she was about to commit an even bigger sin.

She turned her head to look at Quincy. His expression was hard to read, but his eyes were wide open windows. There was lust in their moss-colored depths.

"The couch, I think," she said.

He didn't have any trouble interpreting her meaning. "Might be easier for me to get there if you untied me."

She frowned.

He arched a devilish eyebrow. "You'll want my hands free. I'm not just looking for a way to get free, girl."

She didn't know why she liked him calling her that, but she did. Maybe it was the gruffness in his voice. It made her think of other things that might be a little rough about him. She swallowed the saliva pooling in her mouth then moved behind him and quickly untied the knots. The clothesline slithered to the floor, and he shot up from his seat.

But not to run away. Not to grab her. He held

his pants while he toed off his hiking boots then shoved down his jeans.

Her head got a little dizzy looking at his hairy, muscled thighs and the full-sleeve tattoo that covered his right arm. Then he drew the tee over his head and tossed it away. When he faced her, he was completely nude, and he held still while her gaze roamed over his body.

"My wallet," he said. "Unless you have a rubber."

She moved to her table and picked up his wallet, feeling inside one of the slots for a condom wrapper. Once she handed it to him, she stood still.

"Your turn," he said, his gaze on her body and jerking his chin to tell her to hurry up.

She pulled off her smock then lifted her tank over her head. She wore a sports bra, not very sexy, but you wouldn't know it from the way his nostrils flared as she scraped it upward, exposing her breasts. Before it cleared her head, his hands were on them, plumping them up and squeezing them. How had he moved so quickly?

"The rest," he said, his glance dropping to her jeans.

She slipped out of her shoes then worked the button free at her waist and unzipped, jerking it open. Maybe he was impatient, because he bent and shoved her jeans down her legs then waited as she stood on the ends, one at a time to free her feet.

Then he leaned toward her, kissed her belly, and dove between her legs. His thumbs parted her folds, and he stroked his tongue between them, pressing into her, and sliding upward to flick against her clit, sending a jolt of electricity throughout her body.

And he hadn't even kissed her yet. She cleared her throat and waited for him to look up at her.

"Right," he said, and stood. The tension in his face honed his cheekbones to sharp blades.

Tamara couldn't quite catch her breath. Staring at all that well-developed muscle and feral intent made her dizzy with need.

He reached out and caught her hand. Then he turned and tugged her after him as he strode toward the couch. Once there, his expression changed, his eyebrows drawing together as though he was unsure what to do next.

But she knew. She reached for his face then

stood on her tiptoes and leaned her breasts against his chest as she kissed him.

His mouth opened, and his tongue thrust between her lips, not a tentative move at all. He dove in, cupping her head to hold her still as he took her mouth.

When he pulled away, his eyelids were half-closed, his nostrils flared. His green eyes were nearly all black with desire. He gripped her waist and turned her, gentle pressure guiding her down to the brown leather couch where she sat while he knelt on the blue handmade rag rug in front of the couch. Sensory details to savor for later.

Then he leaned over her and kissed her mouth again, hard and quick. His hands cupped her shoulders then smoothed over her breasts.

She drew a deep breath and arched, pushing her tits into his palms. He took the hint and lowered his mouth to one beaded crest and sucked on it, drawing gently, and then with more fervor, until she dug her fingernails into his hair to hold him there. He let go of the tip with a loud pop then moved across to the other breast, this time circling his head as he teased her nipple, flicking the tip, then chewing on it, until she parted her legs and raised them to his hips.

But he moved downward, kissing her belly, rimming her bellybutton, before finally arriving at her mound. He anchored her thighs on his shoulders and bent over her sex.

Tamara closed her eyes at the first sweep of his tongue. She felt the release of moisture, heard his groan, and couldn't help but move her hips, grinding against his mouth as he thrust inside her. His thumbs held apart her folds as he lavished her with long slides and pointed thrusts. When he flicked the tip of his tongue against her clit, she cried out and pulled his hair, wanting him to come over her. She needed something more substantial filling up her empty space.

When he drew back, she watched as he cloaked himself and gave his cock a single up and down glide. His gaze locked with hers, and he pulled her down over his lap, so that she straddled his thighs. When she settled with her knees on either side of him, he urged her up and placed his big "knob" at her entrance. Then holding apart her folds, he said, "Now, work your way down, babe."

With a strained laugh, she clutched his shoulders and circled her hips as she drove downward. The pressure had her groaning as she sank, at last taking his head inside her, and taking him deeper as she rose and fell, again and again, her excitement already spiraling. She felt hot all over —her skin flushing with heat, sweat beading on her upper lip, her tender inner tissues tingling with a delightful friction.

When at last their groins met, she rested, leaning her cheek on his shoulder as he petted her hair and smoothed a hand down her back.

"You okay?" he asked, his voice graveled.

"Amazing..." she breathed.

"Think you're ready to move?"

There was a hint of amusement in his voice; she leaned back to give him a smile. "I'm savoring the feel of you."

"I'm okay with that," he said with a wicked smile of his own.

"I'm afraid you're going to have to do all the work," she said, her chest rising and falling faster, because she felt the tightening in her core, the beginning of the end.

"I'm up for it," he murmured.

"Yes, you are," she said, tracing a finger along his cheek and gathering sweat.

"Baby, hold on."

That was all the warning he gave her as he rose and turned, pushing her onto the couch, his cock still deeply embedded. When she tightened her legs around his waist, he braced himself on his arms above her. "It's going to get rough."

Then he began to move, pulling out, pushing forward, his movements slow and steady at first, and then gradually quickening.

She thought she was ready, but he took her breath away. Each hard stroke caused her to gasp. Her head turned side to side, and she began to chant, "Yes, yes, yes—*oh fuck me, yes!*"

She exploded, her arms falling to her sides, her back arching from the couch as wave after wave of pleasure swept outward from her pussy.

Vaguely, she heard his shout, felt him move more quickly, then hold still inside her as he filled the condom that protected them both.

When she opened her eyes, she realized her legs were splayed wide and dangling—off the side of the couch and over the back. And he was grinning down at her.

She frowned, embarrassed by the way she'd lost control. Her jaw had probably been sagging the entire time. Had he counted her fillings?

Quincy swooped down and gave her another kiss. This one sweet. No tongue. "Too rough?"

Yes. But not for the reasons he would assume if she said it out loud. "I should probably clean up," she whispered.

His expression shuttered. Quietly, he withdrew and stood to the side of the couch. He held out his hand to help her up.

Help she needed because her knees felt weak. She gave him a small smile, hurried to her station to grab her clothes from the floor, then walked straight toward the bathroom without giving him another glance. Once inside, she turned on the light and glanced at herself in the mirror. She'd thought this was just for fun. Just because she hadn't had sex in a long time, and this would be harmless. One time only. She'd understood the rules. They were strangers really.

So, why did she feel like crying?

Tamara closed her eyes and drew a deep breath. She'd probably left him very confused. He didn't deserve that. *Pull your big girl panties up.*

She took care of business then cleaned up with a washcloth and dressed. When she let herself out of the bathroom, she glanced around the room. He was seated on her station chair again. Dressed as well. Disappointment flooded her. She'd really enjoyed ogling the man.

Pasting on a smile she knew didn't reach her eyes, she moved toward him. "Sorry about that," she said, trying to sound breezy.

He studied her face. "Did I do something wrong?"

She shook her head. Maybe too quickly. His brows drew together. "No, really. It's me. I'm not used to that." Her gaze went to her feet. "I really enjoyed myself. I guess it scared me a bit how much I liked it."

A finger entered her vision, and he tilted up her face. "Do you think now I've had you that this is over?"

She raised her eyebrows. "Isn't it?"

Before he could answer, a pounding sounded a second before the door at the top of the stairs swung open. And even though she didn't know who had opened the door, she rushed toward the stairs. "Don't let that door close!"

QUINCY STOOD to the side as Reaper and Hook asked Tamara questions about Clay Horner's time with her. He could feel the occasional accusatory glances aimed his way from his two fellow bounty hunters. But he didn't give a rat's ass what they thought about the fact he'd lost Horner's trail and hadn't already gotten a description of Tamara's car and plate number.

He was sure the men knew exactly what had happened during the time he'd been trapped inside the bunker with the pretty beautician. He figured he'd get his ass reamed over the incident, but again, he didn't give a shit.

His buddies had interrupted their conversation, just when he'd gotten to the bottom of what was bothering Tamara. He was pissed. At them. At her. Did she really think he fucked anything with a pussy? He liked her.

Then another thought slithered through his mind. Maybe she didn't want anything more than what they'd already shared.

"We're finished here," Reaper said, his tone a little loud.

That pulled Quincy out of his funk.

"You ready to hit the road?" Reaper asked, giving him a frown.

Quincy nodded. "I'll just a need a minute."

Hook coughed. "We'll be outside. Just to make

sure you don't have any problems with that door again."

Quincy gave him a glare, not looking at Tamara again until the two men exited the bunker. Then he gave her a glare. "I need your business card."

She snorted. "Why? You decide you need a haircut?" She reached out for a card from her table then held it out to him.

His arm shot out and snagged her waist. He pulled her against his chest.

Breathless, she glanced up at him, her eyes wide.

Slowly, he lowered his head. He kissed her, giving her a silent promise she might not be ready to hear. *Wait for me. I'll be back.*

And then he pocketed her card and moved toward the exit. When he reached the door, he wedged the cinder block securely against it, promising himself he'd bring back the parts to replace her old hardware.

Then he glanced across at her. She was touching her lips and staring right back at him.

Whistling to himself, he climbed the steps.

IF YOU ENJOYED this story and want to see what happens next, look for Quincy: Montana Bounty Hunters*!*

New Orleans Nights

Quincy

ABOUT DELILAH DEVLIN

Delilah Devlin is a *New York Times* and *USA Today* bestselling author of romance and erotic romance. She has published nearly two hundred stories in multiple genres and lengths, and has been published by Atria/Strebor, Avon, Berkley, Black Lace, Cleis Press, Ellora's Cave, Entangled, Grand Central, Harlequin Spice, HarperCollins: Mischief, Kensington, Montlake, Running Press, and Samhain Publishing.

ORIGINAL BROTHERHOOD
PROTECTORS SERIES

BY ELLE JAMES

Brotherhood Protectors Series

Montana SEAL (#1)

Bride Protector SEAL (#2)

Montana D-Force (#3)

Cowboy D-Force (#4)

Montana Ranger (#5)

Montana Dog Soldier (#6)

Montana SEAL Daddy (#7)

Montana Ranger's Wedding Vow (#8)

Montana SEAL Undercover Daddy (#9)

Cape Cod SEAL Rescue (#10)

Montana SEAL Friendly Fire (#11)

Montana SEAL's Mail-Order Bride (#12)

SEAL Justice (#13)

Montana Rescue (Sleeper SEAL)

Hot SEAL Salty Dog (SEALs in Paradise)

Hot SEAL Hawaiian Nights (SEALs in Paradise)

Brotherhood Protectors Vol 1

ABOUT ELLE JAMES

ELLE JAMES also writing as MYLA JACKSON is a *New York Times* and *USA Today* Bestselling author of books including cowboys, intrigues and paranormal adventures that keep her readers on the edges of their seats. With over eighty works in a variety of sub-genres and lengths she has published with Harlequin, Samhain, Ellora's Cave, Kensington, Cleis Press, and Avon. When she's not at her computer, she's traveling, snow skiing, boating, or riding her ATV, dreaming up new stories. Learn more about Elle James at www.ellejames.com

Website | Facebook | Twitter | GoodReads | Newsletter | BookBub | Amazon

Follow Elle!
www.ellejames.com
ellejames@ellejames.com

facebook.com/ellejamesauthor
twitter.com/ElleJamesAuthor